Blessed Bastard

A novel of Sir Galahad

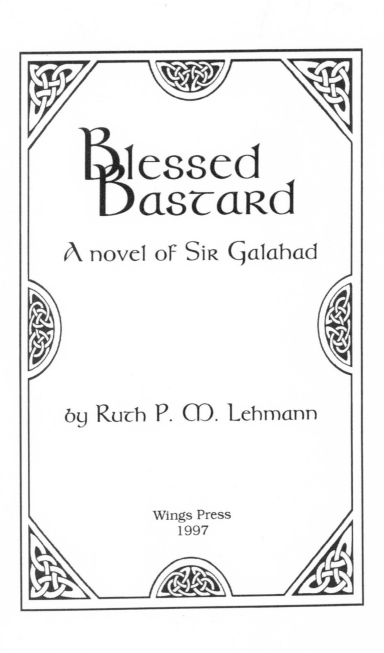

Blessed Bastard

A novel of Sir Galahad

by Ruth P. M. Lehmann

Wings Press
1997

Previously published poems and manuscript locations are cited on page 199.

The cover image, "The Attainment," sometimes known as "The Vision of the Holy Grail," is from a tapestry designed by Sir Edward Burne-Jones and manufactured by Morris & Co. Used by permission of the City of Birmingham Museums and Art Gallery.

Blessed Bastard © 1997 by Ruth P. M. Lehmann

ISBN: 0-930324-35-8

Wings Press
627 E. Guenther
San Antonio, Texas 78210
(210) 222-8449

On-line catalogue and ordering:
http://members.aol.com/wingspress

Contents

Foreword

      I first met Ruth Lehmann in 1978 when I was taking her course in Old Irish language and literature at the University of Texas at Austin. It was an unforgettable class, difficult to be sure, and in some ways, as fascinating as the language we were learning. Ten years later I ran into another veteran of that class – call him John – at Tufts University, where I was teaching early medieval art history. In the interim, John had learned to speak Hindi and Arabic and had worked for an American company in India and along the Persian Gulf. He was now working on a degree in the Fletcher School of International Law and Diplomacy. Now that he could speak Hindi and Arabic, I asked him what he thought of Old Irish. It was still the most difficult language he had ever tried to learn. The publisher of this book, Bryce Milligan, was also a student of Dr. Lehmann. A poet, he has since developed an affinity for Akkadian. Nevertheless, Old Irish remains for Milligan too the benchmark in difficult languages.

      In short, all of us who took that course reached the same conclusion, but not because of the way Ruth Lehmann taught it. Several of the students in the class had studied linguistics with Ruth's husband, Winfred, and were able to approach the original texts, and the structure of their language, from a variety of viewpoints. Known among us as *Frau Doktor,* to distinguish her from her husband, Lehmann's orientation was always that of the master translator. Under her guidance, we learned to achieve serviceable translations of Old Irish prose and poetry into idiomatic English, training which later enabled me to publish scholarly articles applying Old Irish legal, literary and religious texts to early medieval art-historical problems. But while her students groped to simply understand the sense of Old Irish poetry, Lehmann herself produced English translations – years in the making – which employed the same number of syllables per line that she found in the original verse, along with its complex internal rime schemes. That was how we knew that we were in the presence of a master, but her mastery was not simply a matter of technique. While the dust continues to settle from comparatively recent theoretical upheavals, it still seems that literature is more than merely a matter of structure. The members of that class took away with them more than a memory of the difficulty of Old Irish as a language. We each found in its literature something we could have found nowhere else, although what we found differed from student to student.

In *Blessed Bastard,* Ruth Lehmann has set herself several difficult tasks, not unlike those posed by her excellent translations of Old Irish poetry, many of which are incorporated here. Few would attempt a sympathetic treatment of the celibate loner Galahad, and the author's Preface clearly draws distinctions between her own assessment and those of T.H. White and Tennyson, while capitalizing on a few hints in Malory that most of us have missed. Almost annually, new Arthurian novels appear with characters, such as Lancelot and his son Galahad, who only emerged in the literary record in the twelfth or thirteenth centuries, while trying to accommodate the setting to its sixth century origins. But the audience's expectations were codified by Malory in the fifteenth century and Lehmann freely admits the story's need for jousting, tournaments, and their requisite equipment, however unknown these were at a time when Roman Britain was only beginning to become a distant memory.

The translations of Old Irish and Welsh poetry and the characters Lehmann herself introduces bridge the gap. The presence of Caitlín, granddaughter of a lesser Irish king, and the Irish hermit Donnán among the Celtic Britons fits the original sixth century context and offers a comfortable springboard to the poetry, as does the flirtation with Keren, something that humanizes the otherwise unapproachable Galahad while explaining his celibacy. References to the Irish hero Cú Chulainn and the sea god Manannan Mac Lir recall for us that Lehmann's own teacher, Myles Dillon, who was additionally equipped with Sanskrit, was one of those now called "nativists," who mined early Irish literature as a storehouse of pre-Christian, non-classical tradition, while the currently ascendant "anti-nativists" hold that Hiberno-Latin and Old Irish writing developed in tandem, as local variations of the cultural Christianization of early medieval Europe. But wrestling with Galahad's faith leaves Lehmann between the two camps, anticipating the settling of the scholarly pendulum.

This situation is much like that of the "matière de Bretagne" itself, the shrouded origins of which lie in Celtic myth, fragmentary British history, the imaginations of Welsh Bards and French troubadors, and even in apocryphal Gospels. Lehmann's depiction of Galahad's knighting and the Grail quest come ultimately from the Prose *Lancelot* and the *Queste del Saint Graal*, filtered through Malory, but the hermit Donnán reappears, followed by Caitlín, their Irish voices taken intact from the older literature, until Donnán speaks British and it becomes standard English, just as England took over Arthur and made him its own. Camelot remains where it usually is, placed by the West Country accents of the stable boy and the old man defending the apprentice accused by Mordred. Lehmann's rendition of Galahad's combats and the bear hunt are less detached than that of Malory, who did not share Lehmann's sensitivity to Galahad, although he, too, attached importance to dreams. But emotions and the miraculous remain opaque to Malory, while Lehmann looks inside them. Her descriptions of landscapes, seascapes, birds and animals – drawn from her solo walking tours of rural Britain in the 1930s – are more akin to the earlier Celtic literature than the tapestries and stained glass of Malory's time, as readers will discover for themselves in the translations of the older poetry woven into the later tales. This reconciliation of the two traditions, as of father and son, becomes Lehmann's own, as is her insight into the lonely existence of Galahad which is unknown elsewhere. Perhaps the "blessed bastard" will bless Frau Doktor Lehmann for having rescued his character, translating him from a "smug, unbearable creature" into a true hero caught between faith and fate.

– Douglas Mac Lean

Author's Preface

Malory's *Morte D'arthur* is largely a story about Lancelot. Malory gives him the good lines, the exciting action, and manages to use others only to contrast with him. Galahad is in the story to reinforce Lancelot's basic excellence. We never know what Galahad is thinking. Most of his speeches are ceremonial. Trying to remedy this, Tennyson puts in his mouth that undramatic monologue:

> *My good blade carves the casques of men,*
> *My stout lance thrusteth sure,*
> *My strength is as the strength of ten*
> *Because my heart is pure.*

In four lines he makes an inhuman monster of him.

Reading Malory and T. H. White's tales, one sees that the story is basically timeless. White made Guenever into a real woman, and further developed Lancelot, following Malory's interpretation. Malory had greatly narrowed the cast of characters and, as the years go by, only a handful have been assigned a role or an individuality beyond Malory's depiction. Malory shifted incidents, reinterpreted them, focussed the story around a central theme. Although Arthur's building of the court with the best knights of the realm at his Round Table and the fall of that dream is the unifying plan, Arthur is often in the background.

Galahad can be part of that plan without detracting from it. Some of the legends of his upbringing seem consistent with a boy, withdrawn from the central activities of the court and brought up chiefly by a mother steeped in religiosity. White conflated the two Elaines. That and the downgrading of Elaine to a stupid, awkward, fat foil to Guenever is unnecessary. Malory constantly praised her. For Lancelot to choose White's Guenever over this Elaine obliterates Malory's parallel. Between Guenever and Lancelot, even before their love had been expressed in any way, Lancelot could not be lured away even by a young girl of extraordinary beauty – not even after she had borne him a son.

The problem of Galahad is to present a man of whom Lancelot would genuinely be proud, not the little prig that Tennyson created. To that end this story introduces the most appealing of devotional literatures, the Irish. Here not only is there appreciation of the wonder of the world, but often humor. Many of the other traits here, such as Galahad's distaste for killing and his compassion, are hinted at in Malory.

The verse is translated in stanzas imitating the Irish originals in syllabic count, rhythm, rhyme scheme (including special Irish rhymes) consonance, alliteration, and the like. The mood is true to the originals, but though some of these poems might be of the seventh century (the presumed Age of Arthur) most of them certainly are not. All the verses are chosen chiefly for their usefulness to the story.

One problem any treatment of Arthurian legend raises is the history that may lie behind it. Supposedly Arthur as a leader, if not a king, belongs to the sixth century. But at that time the stirrup had not been invented, so lances of a size to knock a man from a horse were not yet practical. Moreover, helmets that covered the whole head also went with the development of cavalry, as did the heavy armor and tall shields used in tournaments. But the accounts we are familiar with were all of a later time. Customs of the court and methods of warfare and single combat were the ones familiar to those who developed this story to their own liking, from twelfth century Geoffrey of Monmouth to fifteenth century Sir Thomas Malory.

The state of England as it is presented here is reasonably consistent with what we know or surmise about Britain a century after the coming of the Anglo-Saxons, though Galahad bears a Norman shield, not a Celtic or Saxon one. The traditional jousting and tournaments are also presented here.

Modern thought also runs counter to much of Malory's. His account depends for interest to a considerable degree on wonders, marvels, and visions besides magic and prophecy. No attempt has been made either to give a literal explanation for everything or to omit the inexplicable, but hints are now and then suggested for the sceptical to develop and the faithful to ignore. As for the rest, if this tale succeeds in rescuing Galahad from the smug, unbearable creature that some of the Victorians and later generations have made of him, then this work will have fulfilled its purpose.

A note on the comb of Chapter 5: the carver of walrus tusk uses the names as they appear in the "Sickbed of Cú Chulainn, or the One Jealousy of Emer." It reads:

> *Fann ingen Aeda Abrat Fann*
> daughter of Aed Abrat

> *ben Manannain maqi Lir*
> wife of Manannán son of Ler

The artist knew ogam and uses the archaic form *maq(q)i* that occurs on some of the standing stones. To be consistent, he should have written Manannani and Leri, but he uses rather the forms of his own day.

Ruth P. M. Lehmann
Austin, Texas

Chapter 1

Loneliness

Wolde God that it were so
As I coulde wishe bitwixt us two.
The man that I loved altherbest
In all this contree, est other west,
To me he is a strange gest;
What wonder est thou I be wo?

Middle English lyric

he moon and stars shone clear in the cool night. The mist wandered in wreathes and wraiths along the line of river beyond the trees. It was yet too early in the year for nightingales or even cuckoos, but the quivering cry of a little owl shivered in the stillness. Within the castle a child was crying alone. Heavy drapes darkened the room where he lay, and in the gloom he wailed.

As his cries grew louder, Dame Brisen came in, shading a candle in her skinny hand. "Hush now, child," she said in her crisp tones. "Your mother is at her prayers. If you disturb her, I'll give you the flat of my hand." The child well knew the sting of those bony fingers. He paused, then the wail changed to sobs, long shuddering sobs of frustration and isolation.

When Elaine had finished her prayers and looked in on him, he was still awake, but the sobs had died away. Elaine pulled back the drapes from the window and the moonlight streamed in across the floor to the foot of the bed. "Thank you, mamma," said a little voice. Elaine stooped over him.

"What, still awake?" Elaine said. "You were very naughty. Now go to sleep. You want to grow up big and strong like Daddy, don't you?"

Elaine's voice was soft and pleasant, not like Brisen's, but it had little intimacy. It was as if her mind were elsewhere.

"Why doesn't Daddy live here?" the little one asked, more to keep her with him talking than for interest in the answer he had heard before.

"You know why," she said. "There is a great lady who simply won't let him. Now go to sleep." Her voice had an edge of bitterness, and he knew now she would go, but she paused.

"When you are lonely," she said, "you can pray as I do. God always listens."

She went out and in the moonlight Galahad at three years old prayed himself to sleep.

In the light of morning frost lay on the blue-green grass like the bloom on a plum. Shadows pointed long fingers from every grassblade, twig, and tree. A robin sang just outside, and a starling whistled. Dame Brisen thought the early hours were healthy and had waked Galahad at dawn and set him out in the courtyard. He had glimpsed his mother entering the chapel. Galahad would have preferred to sleep, but the air was sweet, the birdsong glad, and now he was awake he trotted over to the stables where the grooms were fetching fodder for the horses.

Those great-footed, muscular stallions, strong enough to carry a six-foot man in full armor, towered like giants above the little fair-haired boy. Everyone told him to beware lest he be stepped on and not to touch them and to keep out of the way and not to bother the groom, and above all to watch out when they were saddled for it always made them restless with anticipation.

But Galahad had found a strange fascination here. Today as he watched them shouldering each other as they crowded to the manger or pushed their muzzles deep in the waterbucket, sucking up noisy drafts and slobbering as they

lifted their heads again, one of the largest suddenly threw up his head, whinnied shrilly, and
began to stamp and try to rear. The groom rushed
up shouting, "Ho, there, ho!" When he saw the
child, he was terrified. "Out o' there, young 'un.
It's 'eard that gadfly. Out o' there 'fore 'e kills thee."

Galahad clasped his hands and whispered,
"Please God, help the poor horse." At once the
snorting, rearing monster stood still, shook himself, and went calmly back to munching hay.

The terrified groom stopped shouting and
stared. "It flew out again," said the boy. "I saw it
go."

"Well, get on back fer breakfast. It's na safe
fer thee 'ere." The groom took him firmly by the
shoulders and marched him out to the courtyard.

Galahad wandered into the kitchen. It was
the servants' quarters and Dame Brisen had told
him a dozen times to keep his distance from such
like or he'd get no respect, but it was warm and
the cook was a fine plump motherly soul who
smelled of flour and spices and talked incessantly
and unintelligibly. Everyone there spoiled him and
called him "master" and didn't order him about.

Now he crowded to the warmest end of the
settle in the chimney corner, and they dipped him
a bowl of porridge from the steaming kettle on the
hob and fetched a horn cup of milk with only two
flies in it. He helped them out and they walked
gratefully away, trailing drops of milk across the
worn slab of the table.

As he ate the warm spoonfuls of porridge,
the room was filled with voices. The cook was

muttering to herself in a long monologue as she mixed bread in one corner. Elsewhere there was the usual, "I says to 'im" followed by "an' 'e says to me." But farther away a discussion grew louder and he could not help listening, nor could anyone else except the cook, who was more interested in her own mumble.

The new discussion had to do with "the best knight of the world" and "how does that king let it go on?" and "you can't say e's our maister; 'e ain't never 'ere." Then one put in: "But I 'ear a's been mad these two years, mebbe more. Ya think 'a's cured o' that other madness o' 'is?" Another commented, "But what a maister, e'en if'n 'e's mad!"

Then the cook broke in as if she had heard every word, and she spoke quite clearly: "That little boy, 'e's our maister."

His mother don't do nothin' but pray and moon about; and that Brisen, why she's a hard uncomfortable person no one would gi' the time o' day to." Then they noticed that the boy was listening. Suddenly everyone was silent for a moment, then broke forth louder than ever, some singing, some just laughing nervously, the cook muttering again.

Galahad drained the horn of milk, slipped off the bench and ran out into the sunshine.

When Galahad was six his father had come to stay. The first time he had seen him, he was hollow-eyed, emaciated, never speaking. That had been at Castle Corbin where his grandfather, King Pelles lived. After a month of nursing by Elaine, he had joined them at Castle Bliant, renaming it

Joyeux Gard. The boy watched him shyly – a tall, lean figure, gaunt, hollow-eyed and silent. Elaine had smiled and sometimes sang happy songs, not just: "My lefe is faren in londe," or sacred songs. Galahad liked the songs of Jesus and Mary best, for even when they were sad, a hope lay in the words and his mother smiled as she sang. Now for a week or two Elaine spent less time at her prayers and played more with the boy.

Galahad was moved out of the chamber next to his mother when his father came, and now slept across the hall where he could look out on the courtyard and the battlemented tower opposite. On moonlight nights he could see his father pacing there under the wide sky and looking ever away into the distance. On rainy nights he could hear his footsteps striding restlessly the length of his chamber. Once when his own door was left ajar, he heard his mother sobbing in her room.

He remembered lonely nights of his own and went to her.

"Mamma, why are you crying? Would you like to pray with me?"

She sat up. "It is late. I'm sorry I waked you," she said.

He persisted. "I thought you'd be happy when Daddy came. Aren't you happy, Mamma?"

"You'll know some day," she told him, "that a man can give a woman the greatest happiness in the world – and the deepest hurt. It seems we can't have the one without the other."

"Are you hurting now? Would a prayer help?"

"Yes," she smiled, "I think it would."

They knelt side by side and she prayed to Mary and her Son, asking forgiveness for her faint heart and evil thoughts.

She ended with a prayer to the Virgin, thanking her for this little son. It had been rather a long prayer, but Galahad felt peace and warmth, and his mother smiled after the Amen, when she kissed him goodnight.

His father with that hungry, haunted look of his went riding every day. The big stallion was his favorite mount, and Galahad soon found that if he were careful to be under foot when the great beast was brought out from the stable that Lancelot would swing him up to the saddle in front of him. After a week or two, moreover, his father sent the groom out to catch one of the ponies on the moor. Daily for weeks the pony was being trained for saddle and bridle, and Galahad was never sent from his stall at feeding time, but he was encouraged to feed him and groom him as much as a little boy could.

But all the while the boy saw to it that he did not miss the rides with his father. Those strong, gauntleted hands and the muscular arms about him were safe and warm. He saw too that his father looked for him to join him, waited talking to the groom if he were late coming. Dew was on the grass when they set out with the sparkle of a thousand diamonds on the sward, in the branches of the willows along the river, and like pearls in the wheel-webs of spiders.

When Lancelot had wanted to teach him hawking, the boy had refused. "It is a great sport," his father had urged. "They are beautiful birds. Just look at him!" The peregrine sat proudly on his wrist, his head encased in a plumed hood.

"Hawks are beautiful," said Galahad, "when they fly high and wild. But doves are my friends too, and helpless. Look at the herons, stalking on the river's edge, or flapping so heavily they are easy prey. I don't like killing."

"But lad," protested the knight, "how can you grow up to be the best knight in the world if you won't kill?

The boy thought a moment. "If I must, I shall kill, but I'll get no pleasure from it."

Lancelot never took a hawk while the boy rode with him. At the castle he produced a seax, taken from a Saxon who had fallen. It was short enough and light enough for the boy to handle, and his father set him to practicing every day after their ride. Even at six the boy made steady progress, learning to make no wide sweeps with his arm that would expose him, learning to recover quickly from a lunge at the leather bag. When the pony was trained, Galahad began riding at a halfsize quintain with a little spear. He was small enough to duck as the other arm swung at him after a blow, but his father insisted he must sit upright and move quickly if he were to learn to joust like a man.

All this seems pushing a child through youth too soon in these days of longer and longer years of irresponsibility. But in those days at twelve some were already entering battle, and the arts of combat must be thoroughly learned. Moreover, Galahad heard everywhere from everyone that his father was the "best knight of the world." But only in his seventh year had his father come, a haggard, lonely man, who had stayed away so long from a lovely, lonely woman in a lonely castle – ironically named Joyeux Garde – with a lonely boy. All his mother offered him for company was prayer. As he grew, the feeling of the presence of God became increasingly persistent, increasingly comforting.

Galahad felt uneasy about his father. He intruded into his world, upsetting its routine. His mother had at first seemed really happy, but then had withdrawn even farther, though Lancelot lingered on. But Lancelot had supervised the boy's training; they had walked together, ridden together, and sometimes eaten together. And yet the boy resented him. Would the "best knight in the world" bring sorrow to everyone? Present or absent the knight was the source of overwhelming gloom and yearning, and in his eyes anyone might read his own deep trouble against which he was powerless.

So the days went by and the wild grasses sprouted, faded and curled faintly red in sworls on hillsides where fat deer fed at dusk. Elaine rarely appeared. The boy now rode his pony well and handled the seax with surprising skill. He could make a clean hit at the quintain and gallop on past, unshaken in the saddle. With a bow and arrow he could hit a mark at twenty paces, at least in the target if not in the heart. His bow was too small to send an arrow farther and he had to aim the width of two fists above the target for the arrow to reach it.

Lancelot now and then rode forth. He was calling himself the Chevalier Mal Fet and wandering knights occasionally challenged him. Sometimes these encounters took place within sight of the castle and everyone crowded to the battlements to watch Lancelot tumble someone from his horse. One meeting usually sufficed, and rarely was there a second conflict with swords. Galahad had tried occasionally to swing his seax while mounted, but he found that no easy matter. He appreciated his father's easy control of horse and sword.

Maple trees had turned crimson, the leaves had fallen, and there was ice along the river's edge and on the moat. Still occasionally Lancelot answered a challenge. One day a knight approached, and when Lancelot had crossed the drawhridge, they had merely parleyed. Galahad, who was watching at the gate, heard some part of their talk.

The stranger had said, "You call yourself the Chevalier Mal Fet?" When the other had replied, he added, "I think you are Sir Lancelot."

Lancelot spoke very clearly: "It I were Lancelot and I called myself the Chevalier Mal Fet, don't you think it would be because I did not wish to be known as Lancelot?"

The other saluted. "Indeed, your secret will be safe with me." He had started to say more, but Lancelot returned the salute, his horse swung about, and trotted back across the drawbridge.

Elaine had stepped from the chapel as the two met. She could not hear what they said, but Galahad saw a look of fear or hurt in her eyes as she watched Lancelot return his horse to the stable.

"Will you go?" she asked as he crossed back across the courtyard.

"No," said he, "where should I go?"

"She will send for you."

He looked down at the steps as they entered the wing of the castle with the living quarters. His smile was bitter, and though he tried to keep his voice steady, one heard the ring of despair as he said, "No, she will not."

Spring came and the forest floor was blue with hepaticas and violets. By the edges of clearings primroses, like pale gold coins, were tossed among lichened rocks. Along the river daffodils gladdened the banks with shining yellow. There had been few challenges of late. Word had it in the village that one might as well tilt with Lancelot as with the Chevalier Mal Fet, and being tumbled on the grass has little to recommend it.

But one day two men rode up. One wore no armor, and the other had his visor open and no weapon with him. Lancelot had run to meet them and grasp their hands. For the first time Galahad heard him laugh aloud as he welcomed each, embracing them warmly when they had dismounted. Galahad saw his mother greet them at the top of the steps. She spoke the proper words. She tried to smile. But when they had entered the dining-hall, she all but ran to the chapel, and Galahad saw tears in her eyes as she passed him. She was long at her prayers.

Galahad inconspicuously slipped in with the men and curled up with one of the great hounds by the hearth. The dog had stood up and given a perfunctory "woof," but seeing Lancelot accompanying the men, he had lain down again with a sigh.

"The king has searched the whole island for you," said one knight. "We heard you were mad; we heard you were dead; we heard you had gone abroad."

Said the other: "The queen kept sending knights out whenever one came back without you. She even sent to France and Brittany, but it was soon clear that the trail, even the rumors, ended at the coast."

"Actually," added the first, "she was the one who guessed you might be here."

"We should have known it all along," put in the other.

"Perhaps she did," said Lancelot.

"Oh, no indeed," cried his guests. "She was truly frantic. She has grown very thin and there are deep shadows under her eyes. Arthur is genuinely worried about her. He has called in leeches and asked them for sleeping potions for her. There was fear for her very life or sanity. The whole court has been anxious for her."

By now the servants had brought mugs of warm spiced wine, trenchers of bread, and a bowl of the meat dish from the night before. Lancelot joined the men in drinking the wine and plied them with questions about the friends he had left. He did not ask about the queen, though he asked much of King Arthur and of his successes or setbacks in the north. His hunger for news made clear to the boy the depth of loneliness that had hollowed and lined that handsome face.

Before the boy could slip away, his father caught sight of him. "Here, lad, I want you to meet my friends." The boy stepped obediently forward and bowed. "What do you think, Percival, Ector?"

"He favors you," said Percival. "I'd know anywhere he was your son."

"He seems quiet, more like his mother," said Ector. "What is his mettle?"

"He is quiet,"said Lancelot, "and he is more like her at heart than like me. But he is young. Even now he will not do what he thinks wrong, not for my sake, not for my command. It is as if some inner voice is all he listens to. But he is learning how to handle weapons already."

"Perhaps like his mother he is quiet and yet knows a trick or two," suggested Ector. "If so, he'll find a way to get whatever he wants – by guile, if no other way."

Galahad looked sharply at him. His mother deceitful? She seemed to him detached, unworldly, uninterested in anything of this life – except his father. Was that it?

But now the men had turned to other talk and Galahad slipped out into the sunshine, took his pony and rode along the river where mudhens were peeping in the reeds and now and then a mallard exclaimed loudly about the course of affairs. A harrier skimmed above the marsh grasses and a kingfisher, like a blue-green jewel flashed away upstream. The boy spurred the pony to gallop harder than ever before, almost as if he wished to blot out his thoughts with physical activity, but as soon as he saw the pony was really tiring, he turned back and let it go its own pace. It would never lag on the homeward way, and yet at the slower pace he could sort things out.

His father would return to Camelot, and his life would once more move between lonely prayers and a perpetual feeling of being useless and unwanted with a great deal expected of him that he would never accomplish. But no. His father had changed things in ways that would not return to the old routine. He had the pony so that he had a place in the stables now. At the half-size quintain he could always practice. Handling the seax and shield needed practice too. There were older boys whom Lancelot had coached so that Galahad could get other practice. With them the boy used a wooden sword as they did. Moreover, he had soon found that he could force them into a corner with a natural skill that their greater height and years did not fully compensate for.

Besides this, Elaine had for some months back engaged her priest to give the lad regular lessons in reading and writing. The boy had been adept at this too, and was beginning to find reading as good a cure for loneliness as prayer. But at prayer he had always that glowing sense of God's presence. As he trotted into the stable and helped the groom rub down his pony he thought: "Perhaps if father goes he will take loneliness from us all." But just then Elaine emerged from the chapel and he saw the lost look in her eyes.

At dinner two nights later for the first time in his life Galahad glimpsed court grandure. They ate in the great hall and the trestle tables were set up and scrubbed before noon. Lancelot and his friends had gone hawking on that first day and this morning they had gone out in the glimmering gray before dawn and had caught three fat does, the sweetest, tenderest of meats. Galahad had refused to accompany them on either expedition and had wept over the ducks and doves that covered the table and still more at the four little orphan fawns they had brought back. But these were penned next to his pony and he could teach them to drink from a bucket as he had seen lambs and calves taught.

At sunset tapers and torches were ensconced along the walls of the great room and tables were piled with food. At first Galahad was reluctant to eat, but such odors! Thyme, wild marjoram, basil, and fennel; onions and garlic and horseradish. There were steaming broths and gravies and roasted, stewed, and baked meats – too recognizable for the boy's liking, but wonderful to taste. He sopped his bread in broth to begin with, but then his father put a bit of venison on his plate and soon he was reaching and grabbing and gnawing away with the rest of them.

Beer and wine flowed freely with the meal and laughter rang out. The hounds quarreled for scraps of gravy-soaked bread under the table. The rushes, fresh laid on the floor that afternoon, were greasy now with bones, but still gave a freshness to the hall, aided by new pine branches at the doors, the fragrance of which chased the mustiness of disuse from the room. Servants kept plates filled and cleared away plates of bones, careful to see that platters were not wholly empty when they replaced them with fresh ones.

      Elaine sat with a serene smile – at least her lips smiled below the empty eyes. After the men sat back and held their sides, stuffed with good things, she rose, filled a brimming goblet with mead and offered it to her father, others to Sir Percival, Sir Ector, and to Sir Lancelot. At the far end of the table a bard stood up, swept his fingers over his harp, and chanted an old song of the boy Arthur, plucking a sword from a stone. Another singer bowed his crowd, and to that thin music sang of Easter and the opening of the empty tomb. There were songs of Siegfried and of Theodoric that a Saxon minstrel sang, and then the first bard chanted of the great deeds of Lancelot and of the court at Camelot. Amid this Galahad fell asleep and was carried off to bed. He heard his mother come to her room not long after, but the sounds of joy still rang out below across the angle of the courtyard. Galahad waked as the gray of dawn glimmered. He heard men's heavy and not always steady footsteps in the hallway passing his door to proceed to the guestrooms beyond. Someone paused outside his door, then voices as Elaine opened her door told him his father was there.

"You will go," she said softly, "but when?"

"Yes, I must," he said. "She has sent for me. But I cannot expect them to leave today." Galahad understood, as did Elaine, that he meant "I cannot leave soon enough, but my guests must sleep." He added, "About this hour tomorrow we'll set out."

There was a slight pause, then Elaine said, "Thank you for this year, but of course you must go. God bless you. Your son and I will remember you in our prayers."

"My dear," said Lancelot – the first word of tenderness he had used to her – "should I ever find heaven, I shall know whom to thank."

Lancelot went to his room and when both doors had closed Galahad lay awake wondering. He did not think his father loved his mother, and Percival had spoken of her guile. His mother, he was sure, loved his father – loved him more than she loved anyone but God. But guileful? Then he thought of Dame Brisen. Surely that was the clue. He had heard a whisper in the kitchen that she was a witch.

Chapter 11

Deceit

I must go walke the wood so wild,
And wander here and there
In dred and dedly fere,
For where I trusted, I am begild,
And all for oon.
Thus am I banisshed from my blis
By craft and false pretens,
Fautles without offens,
As of return no certen is,
And all for fere of oon.

Middle English lyric

alory tells of how Galahad was conceived. There was more to it than Dame
Brisen's whim. First, it had been predicted, and who would cross the fates?
Second, Elaine had been bound in a
most painful enchantment – or so they said. For
years she was burning with fever, then bathed in
perspiration, followed by chills that defied all heat
to warm her. Then the fever would set in again,
and the drenching sweats and more chills. They
described it as if she were immersed in boiling
water. Actually hot baths, cold baths, tepid baths
had been suggested as treatment. Nothing availed.

Then came Lancelot to her father's castle,
all unsuspecting that he was riding straight into
the web of destiny. He merely had to hold out his
hand to the lady and her fever dwindled to a pleasant warmth, and the lovely young girl took his
hand and stepped out of the water. From that
moment she loved him, everlastingly, inescapably.
Her father, King Pelles, who had so long been helpless before her misery, decided to act, now when
he could help her. Dame Brisen was a ready ally.

Elaine was beautiful, pure, and young. A
couple of years earlier, Lancelot would have married her at once. But now he had progressed from
respecting Arthur's queen and admiring her
beauty to finding that he thought and dreamed of
little else. Indeed, the quest he had pursued that
had brought him to Castle Corbin where he rescued Elaine, he had undertaken to escape from
the frank friendship in Guenever's eyes and the
glorious light of her red-gold hair. Without magic

or destiny he had fallen as desperately in love as Elaine, and it seemed to him then, as miserably, as hopelessly, for she was his queen. He had sworn allegiance to her husband, a king he loved in true friendship. Honor as well as the church forbade that he and the queen ever, ever speak of love.

But on that night of the rescue, Dame Brisen came to him. It was dark and he had paid no attention to her during the day, so that he accepted it when she said she came from the queen. Had he been less self-assured, he should have doubted her message that the queen awaited him not far away. They had not spoken of love; he had only his arrogance to make him think that the queen would ever betray her husband. Yet he followed Dame Brisen a couple of miles, his horse snorting and annoyed at having to find his way through the total darkness of a night without moon or stars.

Up in the tower dark curtains that hung from ceiling to floor shaded the narrow, shoulder-high window, set deep in the thick stone wall. Lancelot could see nothing. Dame Brisen paused outside the door and whispered, "There is a bed to the right, an ell from the door. She is expecting you."

Trembling with the wonder of it – a dream that had so often made him long for sleep to bring it, as it frequently had – he pushed open the door. Could that hope, that dream now be unfolding in reality? She was there? She was awaiting him? Darkness and silence in that lonely tower – and the dream.

It was full daylight and Lancelot had drawn back the curtains to enjoy the beauty of her broad brow and softly curling hair. There in the bed was the child Elaine, holding the blankets up to her chin and looking at him fearfully and adoringly. Lancelot strode to the bed and jerked the blanket from her hand. She curled there in the great bed, naked as when he had raised her from the water.

"Please forgive me," she faltered. "They predicted I would bear your son. They said it must be. He is destined to be the best knight of the world. Even you, my lord, will not quite reach his perfection."

"But he was conceived by guile, yet with thoughts of a greater sin. How can there be perfection in that?"

Elaine had regained the blankets by this time, and her father and Dame Brisen (who must have been listening at the door) stepped into the room. "God moves in mysterious ways," said King Pelles. "We must do His will and not thwart His wishes. Ourself would be happy to welcome you as our son. Will you let us celebrate your marriage?"

"You assume too much," Lancelot growled between clenched teeth. He tightened his tunic about him, swept up the rest of his clothes in one hand, and withdrew to the attiring room where he pulled on his clothes as quickly as he could, and left the tower at once without a farewell or a return to the castle for sword or shield.

The memory of that night and what he had thought it had been made him greet Guenever with shining eyes that read in her smile of delight at seeing him again the conviction that his dream might at last come true. Soon, indeed, there came a time when Arthur was called to a parley in the north and asked Lancelot to remain in case there were trouble in the east. From then on Lancelot and Guenever felt alive only in each other's presence.

But that was not all, for Elaine, too, was in love. The child was a lovely plump baby that ate and slept and grew and rarely cried. Elaine was a devoted mother, eager that the baby have the best of care. She refused to have a wet-nurse looked for and insisted on feeding him herself as very few mothers of her rank did. She felt that perhaps there was a special virtue in her, since all this had been decreed. Moreover, she felt that a healthy, adorable child would be irresistible. To that end she nurtured him. His father had been named Galahad Lancelot, though no one used his first name. She called the boy after him, and when he was a year old, she dressed in her best, took the child in a scarf slung from her shoulder, and with Dame Brisen as companion set out for Camelot. Through the warmth of the day her palfrey paced smoothly down the road with hawthorn hedges in bloom on either side, and Brisen jogging behind on a quiet mule. As the sun set, they reached the town.

The next day she presented herself at court. Before she arrived word had got about that this was Elaine, daughter of King Pelles, and that the child with her was Lancelot's son. The queen had wondered what to do. Of course she was hurt. She knew that in theory one cannot command love, but it is never easy for a woman of perfect beauty, and especially for a queen, to know how much another feels for her admiration, pride of possession, or obligation not to thwart her wishes. Love, respect, interest in her for herself, these Guenever could never be sure of. She must know what Lancelot thought of Elaine, how all this had come about. She sent for him. He had not yet seen Elaine, but he had heard she was there with the child. Lancelot was cautious and formal when he was summoned to the queen's presence. But he omitted the title as a conciliatory gesture, respectful, but neither abasing nor distant.

"My lady," he began, bowing low, "you wished to speak with me?"

"I would know," she said, picking her words carefully, "is there truth in the claims of this young woman who has arrived with a child?"

Lancelot would not quibble. "My most dear lady," he said, "there is truth in the claim that I am father of the child she calls Galahad. But she is not my wife, and I have no intention to make her so or ever to live with her under any arrangement."

"It must be nearly two years ago when you – err– met her," said the queen, not looking at him. "You told on your return of rescuing the daughter of King Pelles from enchantment. Is this she?"

"Yes, I was asked to lead her from the boiling vat."

"And then? She was grateful, I suppose, and inexperienced."

"That is true. Moreover, she and her father were convinced that the child of us two would be the best knight of the world, better than his father. Together they plotted to deceive me."

"But how?" asked the queen. "You are no child."

Lancelot's voice was very low as he replied, "I was told that you awaited me."

Her nostrils flared as she quickly drew in her breath, and her cheeks flushed darkly. Her voice had an edge now. "Two years ago I had never summoned you. You had no right to think I might. How could you be so duped?"

"It will not happen again, your majesty."

"No, so you may hope. But tonight I shall send for you when you least expect it, and if you are not in your chamber, I shall know that either you are a two-fold fool or you have lied about her."

As Guenever uttered these last words, Dame Brisen entered. When the queen finished she stepped forward and announced Elaine.

Elaine was dressed in scarlet, gold and flame – rather too brilliant for her pale beauty. Her costume clashed like the slash of a blade running red with the purple, blue, and green of Guenever's mantle and gown, a costume made bright by the thick golden braids that hung down to sweep her knees. Elaine's hair was caught back in a coif that concealed it. Lancelot drew back as she approached, but she did not glance at him. She came straight to the queen and knelt before her, setting Galahad at her feet.

The child crowed and smiled, his hair like thistledown. The queen smiled too, though there was pain in that smile. The barren queen had no child, and never would have. But she accepted childlessness as she had accepted her father's managing of her betrothal to Arthur, whom she had come to admire and love, and as she had accepted, however reluctantly, that passionate love of Lancelot.

"Do we have permission to tarry a day or two, your majesty?" Elaine murmured.

The queen clapped her hands and a lady-in-waiting stepped forward and courtesied. "Show the daughter of King Pelles to the chamber I spoke of," she ordered.

Elaine gave one quick glance at Lancelot as she lifted the child and followed the lady-in-waiting out of the hall. Lancelot had not looked at her.

"It was not necessary," he said to the queen.

"Perhaps not," she replied, "but it was kind. Young Galahad is a child to be proud of." She was looking steadily at him and she read in his face – if she was not deceived – that this woman, and even this dear young life, were principally an embarrassment to him.

The room Guenever had selected for Elaine was next to her own. Usually it was empty or one of the waiting women slept there. Occasionally the queen had made use of it, for Arthur's room was just beyond her own.

It was past midnight when Lancelot heard

the timid knock. A small figure – she was barely twelve years old – came in with a candle and whispered, "She would like you to come." Lancelot was already in his robe. He followed her flickering candle along the corridor. He had seen the girl the last few days about the queen. She was the daughter of one of her dearest and oldest ladies-in-waiting. The candleflame did not reveal the red and gold girdle about the girl's waist, a girdle Elaine had worn that very afternoon. Nor did he see Dame Brisen draw back into the shadows as he stepped into the corridor.

In the royal apartments the girl stopped at a door and rapped, then pushed the door open. Lancelot knew the room, its curtained bed opposite the door between high windows, shaded lest the candle be visible outside. The bed held a smooth young form, and he slid in beside it, his robe slipping to the floor.

Before daylight he was gone again, and soon was stretched in his own bed, deep in happy dreams. The messenger from the queen had come and gone on a fruitless search.

About ten the next morning the queen asked him to attend her. He found Elaine and Galahad with her, all three standing by a tall window that let in a glory of light. Castles were mostly dark and frequently damp, but here up until noon the light streamed across the floor.

Guenever was pale and she spoke with unusual formality. "Sir Lancelot," she said, "thy wife and child plan to return to Corbin Castle. I suggest that thou escort them."

"But your majesty," he began, imitating her formality, "they came unescorted, they may go unescorted; and though he is my child, she is not my wife."

"Why wert thou not in thy room when I sent for thee?" she asked. She used "thou" not in her accustomed tone of familiarity, but as master to servant.

Bewildered, Lancelot looked wildly at Elaine. Her head was bowed; he could not see her face.

"Thy lady hath confessed that thou hast spent much of the night with her. Canst thou deny it?"

Lancelot groaned a shuddering, heart-rending moan. But the queen in her pain had no mercy. "Go," she said. "Go with her or without her, but thou needst never return."

"Mother of God," he cried, "twice a fool!" With that he leapt through the window into the bushes below, his face a mask of pain. At that cry Galahad wailed aloud and the women glared at each other.

"Your majesty," said Elaine, tense and despairing, "I am not his wife. He cares less for me than for one of his hounds or for one of the shoes of your feet. I tricked him, or rather Dame Brisen tricked him, by the same strategy that was successful before. In the dark he could not know. I spoke as little as I could and only in a whisper."

"How could you hope to win him by such means?" asked the queen.

"There was always hope – until now," she

replied. "Now he is lost to us both. He is mad; he hates himself; he may destroy himself or egg on others to destroy him. I have been wrong and selfish, but I think my love was greater than yours. I would not have hurt him and sent him to his death."

"We are both wrong," said the queen, "Now we must accept the bitterness of love."

Galahad wailed louder as his mother began to sob. The queen stood silent, tears welling in her eyes and coursing down her cheeks. She turned to the window. A broken spray of the rose that had checked Lancelot's fall lay on the grass, two blossoms crushed where his heels had ground them into the soil. But the proud form had disappeared across the drawbridge and into the forest.

When Elaine returned to her father, he could read the misery in her eyes. It was then he gave her the nearby castle called Bliant. There was little joy in those empty rooms, but much as he wished her by his side, King Pelles sensed how she must loathe his own home where for so long she had suffered that evil enchantment, or illness.

Elaine had been a loving and devoted mother up until that ride to Camelot. Afterwards she spent more and more time at her prayers, leaving the boy to Dame Brisen. So he grew up without love or companionship, a lonely boy in a lonely castle with little comfort, except for the God he prayed to and walked with.

Then to Corbin Castle Lancelot had at last come. His madness had shut out all thoughts that gave him pain, all recollection of who he was or where he had been. Armor and weapons, horses and hawks, all the trappings of a knight he shunned. At first he ran naked through the woods and hid from the world, running in fear from every human shape, living with the cattle in the fields. When he was weak for lack of food, sometimes a serf would take him into his hovel if he helped with the haying or apple-picking or spreading dung on the fields. He did not speak; he could not remember his name. All he was aware of was wretchedness and guilt, but not what he might be guilty of.

There were many tales of the wild man of the woods. He was often beaten and mocked, but he refused to protect himself. He defended his head with his arms, crouched in the dust, while stones cut and bruised him. He grew so thin every rib showed and every joint bulged larger than calf or arm above or below it. And the days, weeks, months, years slipped by.

No one knows, least of all Lancelot, how he happened to be asleep under a bush in the rose garden of Castle Corbin. Elaine was visiting her father when they found him. His beard was shaggy, his hair a matted mass. But when Elaine went to see the man asleep there, she knew him at once. She knew because she had hoped so long, and the tales of a wild man in the woods had made her ponder. No one knows how long he slept. It was twelve hours after they had found him, brought him inside, and put him to bed before he waked, Elaine could see he did not recognize her. After baths, hair-trimming, good food, and a week of rest with her sitting beside him, she thought he remembered a little. Gwenever had kept his shield, but had given her his sword to carry back from Camelot. It stood now beside the bed with the sword and shield he had left with her on that first morning when he had rushed from her in anger, so long before.

One day when he was up and dressed, but still had not been outside of the room, Elaine found him looking carefully at the weapons and the device on the shield. He said, "I think these must be mine."

Elaine assured him of this. She was undecided how much information she should volunteer.

"I suppose, then, I must be a knight?'"

"You are a knight of King Arthur's Round Table," she explained.

Lancelot rubbed his forehead as if it hurt. "Gwen," he said thoughtfully, as if the name had occurred to him but he could not place it. Elaine knew that he had no recollection at all of her or of the golden-headed boy she sometimes brought with her to play in his room.

"My lord," she said, "there is nearby a castle my father has given me. If you wish, it is yours."

"Why should I have a castle?" he asked.

"Just as you will," she replied, "but it is there. We might be more at ease there."

And so they went to Castle Bliant that

Lancelot renamed Joyeux Gard. Gradually his recollection returned. She knew, because instead of being always gentle, always humble, he became more and more withdrawn. He had announced one day that he would be called the Chevalier Mal Fet. Shortly after he had the device on his shield painted out, and began sketching designs for it. When he was satisfied, he asked to have it blazoned: a knight kneeling before a lady – argent on a field sable. The lady wore a crown.

It was after that that he began instructing Galahad in handling seax and lance. Before that they had ridden out together for those long rides while the pony was being caught and trained.

Chapter III

Boyhood

Ich am of Irlaunde,
And of the holy londe
Of Irlande.
Gode sire, pray ich thee,
For of sainte charitee.
Come and daunce wit me
In Irlaunde.

Middle English lyric

Now Lancelot had gone again, Elaine withdrew almost completely. She would have entered a convent gladly, but she wanted her son to be well cared for. She looked forward too to the day when he might be acknowledged the best knight of the world. She thought with a little smile that he might one day topple his father from the saddle. Therefore, she encouraged all his exercises in manly sports, she made sure his instruction in reading and religion was never neglected, but she gave little of herself. Galahad was happy, however, that Dame Brisen, too, kept aloof, except to make sure he played with as few children about the castle as possible. Indeed, except for those with whom he practiced feats of arms, she permitted him none.

Then came Caitlin from Ireland. Caitlin was fifteen with bright red hair. Her skin was white and so delicate that it seemed transparent, with a tracery of blue veins showing through its smoothness and a light sprinkling of tiny freckles on her nose. Her eyes were blue-green with long lashes and her forehead broad and smooth. She had been attached to the court of King Mark of Cornwall in the retinue of his Irish queen. In the servant's hall they said that Isolt had sent her to Joyeux Gard because Tristram had looked too long at her.

Tristram had come riding by one day and had passed the night at Joyeux Gard. After dinner he had played his harp and sung songs of Cornwall, Brittany, and Ireland. Caitlin had joined in, sometimes singing one stanza while Tristram replied with another, sometimes one or the other sang, the other joining in the refrain. Galahad asked her about the rumors next day.

"It is good with us, the singing," she replied. "But the queen, it is she in her jealousy. There is that green heart at her."

Galahad laughed at the thought of a green heart, but Caitlin never said the expected. He had once heard Dame Brisen quizzing her about the court in Cornwall, especially about Isolt. "It is great, the beauty on her," Caitlin had said. "Eyes deep blue, rimmed with black, and black the lashes of her. It is she is the beauty, with her dark hair and brows. She is slim and tall with the white grace of a swan, and it arching its neck to smile at a cygnet. But only Tristram gets that straight wide look of her eyes, and she smiling." Mark was a great black hairy man with a gentleness to warm the heart. "But there is no wisdom in him, madam. His wittiest word from one day to the next is his snoring the night between."

From Caitlin Galahad learned the joy of life and laughter and love. The loneliness and pain of love that he had seen all around him his first seven years were swept away in her smiles and songs. The songs were new, and they blended that adoration of the shining earth, its trees, its birds, its fruitfulness with the adoration of God and His angels, as if they were all about one, Caitlin's faith was joyous. It did not withdraw her from the world, but drew all outdoors into her heart.

    Caitlín watched Galahad practicing with his seax, riding at the quintain, and attacking his companions in their sword games. Afterwards she told him, "You it is are the Cú Chulainn." Then she told him how Cú Chulainn at his age had come to Emain Macha where the Ulster king Conchubar lived, and had beaten the three fifties of boys at all their games. He had taken arms on a day that was to make him famous, and had ridden about Ireland in his chariot, bringing home a herd of wild deer and a flock of birds all alive, and the heads of the wicked men bumping on the floor of the chariot. When Galahad said he would not hunt, she had laughed and said, "Then it's alive you shall bring them home, like Cú."

    She told also of how Cú Chulainn at eight years old had killed the great fierce watchdog of Cúlann and had got his name, serving as watchdog until a whelp had been trained to take his place. Galahad, who had made a habit of curling up with the wolfhounds for warmth and affection, felt perhaps he would rather be Cú Chulainn than the best knight of the world. But Caitlín assured him Cú Chulainn was indeed the best knight of the world.

    Galahad told her once of his father – the little he knew of him, and that he had been mad before he came to Joyeux Gard. Caitlín then told him of a king who had gone mad in Ireland at the screams and groans and clashing of swords in a great battle that had lasted for a week. He had run naked throughout Ireland and they said he had grown feathers like a bird and leapt from tree to tree. "Not certain I am about the feathers," she said, "except for the decency of it." Galahad did not join in her laughter as he thought of his father, hollow-eyed, haunted by a dream remote and unattainable. Then she said that the fame of the king was in the songs composed in his madness, and she sang him one.

Tonight the snow is chilling,
filling my cup of sadness;
I have no strength for struggle
at length in hungry madness.

All see I am not shapely,
my tatters hide me poorly:
I am Sweeney of Ros Ercain,
a madman am I, surely.

There comes no sleep with nighttime;
my feet can find no pathway;
I dare not wait here longer:
fear is stronger in halfday.

My aim – to sail out yonder,
crossing the fair main over;
but fear has sapped my courage;
I forage here, mad rover.

Brown branches wounding, cleaving,
my helpless hands are tearing;
the briars have stripped me leaving
no weaving for my wearing.

When Galahad heard that the king had been
befriended by a saint who had a pet wren and
that the king had gone to heaven, he wondered
if his father too might be saved.

   Caitlin was the granddaughter of a king
in Ireland. He was not a great king of a prov-
ince, but he had lands in the west of Ireland
and was important enough to have placed his
children in fosterage at the court. When Isolt
was brought to Tintagel from Ireland, Caitlin's
mother was in her retinue, and she herself was
a child of three or four. Galahad could believe
that she had once been his age. He could not
believe that his parents and certainly not Dame
Brisen could ever have been young. He was glad
that Caitlin had a family of distinction, for otherwise he would not have been allowed to spend
so much time with her. He loved her many
songs, especially one of a hermit and his cat.
Galahad liked its equation of mousing and
study, and the odd arhythmic rhymes (to our
ears) were familiar to him in his native Welsh.

Pangur Bán and I, each bent
on using his own talent:
his heart on hunting will be,
mine on my special study.

Better than fame is knowing,
my book freely following;
Pangur envies not my wish,
he loves his chores though childish.

Two at home, not bored are we,
together ever happy;
each one doing his own thing,
his special skill pursuing.

After brave battles occur
his net may a mouse capture;
in my own net falls as well
a rough rule in sense subtle.

His clear acute eye he sets,
fixed on the fence-wall complex;
I, my own eye, weak yet bright,
I bring to bear on insight.

He is glad to move quickly
with mouse caught in paw-prickly;
I, too, am glad when I plumb
some dear, difficult question.

Though for some time thus we are,
each troubles not the other;
good each thinks his craft to be.
amusing himself only.

Every day he does the work
in which himself is expert;
hard words I make clear and sure;
I too work well like Pangur.

There were other songs, too, bright with the
world around:

Bee flying fast, cup to cup,
sup in sun, hying from home;
fair in flight toward the high heath,
nigh beneath come feast in comb.

Another that showed a touch of displeasure at
the ceremonial bell-ringing of the monks Caitlin
had translated with a giggle.

Ah merle, merry you and well,
what cherry hides nest and all?
Hermit, who will ring no bell,
you sing well your soft, sweet call.

But as if to compensate, she sang another:

Wells of weeping, God me yield,
pay for guilt – venal, revealed–
with no true tear, my own soul
unwhole – a sear, unsown field.

Caitlin was fifteen when she came to
Joyeux Gard and twenty when she left. Galahad
was twelve and he loved her. He no longer rode
the pony, but a light mare, a happy spirited
creature that he called Kate. The girl had returned the compliment by calling her palfrey
Cú for Cú Chulainn, as she had called the boy.
The two often rode together along the forest
trails, leaving undisturbed the bird's nests they
discovered, and pausing to listen to a song-

thrush or nightingale, pouring out his heart. They were such friends that they did not need to babble constantly, but sharing each other's company was enough. As they rode she sang. Some were haunting Irish songs that she could not explain:

Wild wet waves are billowing
across sea-sands thundering,
setting on Conaing alone
in his frail craft sundering.
The hag her white mane lets fling
at Conaing's currach sinking;
a cruel grin curls her lip
at Tortu tree, the magic.

But there were other songs with the happiness of youth:

Dear each new thing, never dull,
young folk's wishes are fickle:
fair the choices love can bring;
sweet the words of youth wooing.

Then when Caitlin was eighteen, Dafydd came to Joyeux Gard. Dafydd was a minstrel who had wandered down from North Wales, singing songs of Taliesin and of heroes and conquests unknown in the south. He could also compose verse on demand to praise a leader or a great lady, and as long as he flattered and amused, he was welcome. At Joyeux Gard he was scarcely noticed except by Caitlin. But he stayed and stayed. It had been a wild rainy evening when he arrived, and it had heralded a week of storm, so it is not surprising that he did not move on at once. After that came the frosts and his horse went lame. Dafydd still remained.

Galahad liked him. He taught him to play the harp, and he taught him new songs. Some of these were hermit songs like those Caitlin sang in Irish. But Dafydd's songs needed no translation. The praise of the changing seasons, the devotion, the love of heaven and earth were in the religious spirit Galahad found closest to his heart. Some too were elegies for princes dead or a vanished way of life or poems of moral counsel, mingled with nature imagery or elegy.

Hall of Cynddylan is gloomy tonight:
no fire, no sleeping
wait awhile after weeping.

Hall of Cynddylan is gloomy tonight:
no fire, no taper –
keep me sane, O my Maker!

Hall of Cynddylan, shapeless you have grown,
your guard in the ground.
Alive he kept your walls sound.

Hall of Cynddylan is gloomy tonight,
no fire, no singing:
grief scores my cheek, tears stinging.

Earn of Pengwern, plumed head gray tonight,
how high its calls hover,
fain for flesh of my lover.

Earn of Pengwern, plumed head gray, tonight,
its scream is high, sullen,
fain for flesh of Cynddylan.

Earn of Pengwern, plumed head gray, tonight,
how high its claw, snarling,
fain for flesh of my darling.

Earn of Pengwern, proudly calls tonight,
on men's blood broodtng:
Trenn is a town deluding.

Earn of Pengwern, proudly calls tonight,
men's gore it's gulping:
Trenn is a town exulting.

Galahad remembered only a few stanzas
of the moral poems:

Fair tops of reeds: mad the jealous:
though rarely to be had,
home is loved by thoughtful lad.

Fair tops of woods: crests shove evenly high,
oak leaves drift down from above:
happy he who sees his love.

Fair tips of cress; horses roam together,
woods sing to one alone;
heart smiles on its love at home.

Dafydd was gentle and kind, but manly and courageous. Some of the men had resented his coming and had tried to pick a quarrel. Dafydd had laughed at first and refused to be serious until he saw how much they were in earnest. Then he had quickly accepted the challenge. He claimed no knightly privileges but accepted their choice of weapons, agreeing to fight with singlesticks. The fight was brief. The challengers were at once out-maneuvred and sent reeling in turn, their heads ringing from resounding blows on their skulls. At the sight of the blood on each other's cheeks, they capitulated, and no one bothered the young Welshman further.

Dafydd told Galahad and Caitlin later that his father had a castle in the north near the coast of Wales, but he was a younger son with little hope of inheriting the estates, though his second brother was in the church. His father was not well, but his eldest brother was getting good experience in managing their holdings. Dafydd, then, had set out with horse and harp to seek his fortune. It seemed he was not to seek farther than Joyeux Gard.

Before Dafydd's coming Caitlin had often joined Galahad at his books, and had learned to read and write along with him. But now for the most part he worked alone. He had looked forward to spring, the streams no longer bound by ice, lambs arriving on every hillside, white and gleaming in contrast to the gray ragged wool of their dams. But if he asked

Caitlin to accompany him, either Dafydd accompanied them or all her talk was of him. Dafydd was clever at all manner of skills. He made harps for them both and taught them to play. He taught them to use a sling to hurl the smooth rounded stones gathered from the swiftest streams. He seemed to know all the songs they did besides many more of Wales and Saxon England. His mother's people lived in Strathclyde, close to the Scottish Gaels, and he knew their songs too.

In this progressive loneliness of the waking year Galahad learned to understand the pain of love that had darkened the world for his father and mother. He had never felt that he owned Caitlin or that she owed him all her attention, and he had known for so long that he could not fill the emptiness in his mother's heart that even this pain as he saw Caitlin turning away from him was dulled. Some little boys with their first attachment might become annoying, demanding, and quarrelsome as they felt the prick of desertion. But Galahad had always known more loneliness than happiness, and recognized that love can be a very selfish pleasure. So he rejoiced in Caitlin's obvious happiness and stored away in his heart the memory that love has an end – human love. He prayed longer now, immersed himself in the Bible, and looked forward to his first official entry into the church, which had been promised him with appropriate laying on of hands for next Easter tide.

Elaine was disturbed when Dafydd asked

her for Caitlin's hand, He had few prospects, and Elaine was uneasy at the position she found herself in – a role that should have been her husband's. But she could see the two were in love, and Caitlin refused to make any demands about what circumstances she would marry into. One day, soon after the beginning of Lent, a messenger arrived, telling of the death of Dafydd's brother, who had been thrown, dragged, and kicked by a horse he was training. At once Dafydd set out for Wales, but now he had Elaine's promise that he might in the summer return for Caitlin.

Everything at Joyeux Gard now turned to preparations for Galahad's initiation into the church. He had sworn a particularly strict abstinence for this Lenten season. He ate no meat, drank only water, and reduced his eating to one meal a day of bread and cheese and watercress. He would have omitted the cheese as the Irish hermits had done, but his mother, approached by the anxious cook, had told him he owed God a healthy and perfect body.

To add to the austerity Galahad considered denying himself Caitlin's company. But then he realized that this would be to deny her the only person she could talk to of Dafydd, and the pain of it to himself made her starry eyes an added penance.

Galahad was not taken into the church at the customary age of seven, for he must go to a bishop for the final rites. A little procession, then, set out for Glastonbury, not far from

Camelot, riding through trails lined with he-
patica, grape hyacinth, and violets with primroses in less wooded sections of the way. They
arrived shortly after sundown. Galahad ate a
supper of bread and water, donned his white
clothes of a candidate, and was conducted to
the church. All night he knelt praying. His
knees, aching and stiff, gave so much pain he
had no trouble staying awake. Other lads,
mostly younger than he, and a couple of older
men who had the fair hair of Saxons kept vigil
with him. They would quietly flex their knees
now and then or walk between the stations of
the cross, kneeling briefly before the little shrine
that marked each. Galahad, however, refused
to move except now and then to gaze at the image of Jesus above the altar that seemed to smile
and beckon in the flickering torchlight.

Galahad noted as the gray of dawn
showed clearer and brighter that the little chapel
was aglow with flowers – blackthorn that the
country people called palm, daffodils, wild flags,
and other lilies – and the air was heavy with
incense and the smoke of guttering candles. By
this time the younger boys were curled asleep
on the cold flags and the older men sagged
against the altar rail, their measured, sometimes noisy, breathing revealing their state of
consciousness. One by one, however, the men
gave a snort that waked them. Each looked fur-
tively about and resumed his prayers.

The sun had not yet risen when a young
priest entered, waked the little boys and told

all to prepare, for the bishop would impose his hands before the other rites of this Easter day. Galahad was the last to approach the altar, for the priest had lined them up as they had begun their vigil, and those from still farther away had spent a night or two there already.

All had been catechized and confessed the day before. Now the bishop came to each, signing his forehead with the cross and anointing him with fragrant oils. To each he said in Latin: "I confirm thee with the sign of the cross, and I confirm thee with the chrism of salvation, in the name of the Father and of the Son and of the Holy Ghost. Amen." Galahad could hear only the murmur of his voice until the bishop approached him. As the cool fingers touched his brow and the odor of balsam came to him with the chrism, he felt a surge of warmth throughout his frame and a sense of total disorientation, as if he had stepped into another world. He closed his eyes and clutched the altar rail. His head pounded and he seemed to hear a choir of angels chanting "Hallelujah!" It was only a moment. Then he rose and looked at the cross. Christ's image was like his father: the hollow cheeks, the large sad eyes. The outstretched arms seemed to embrace the world and His majesty was proclaimed by the jeweled crown on His brow.

In that instant, Galahad had become a man. No longer did he feel anything but gladness for Caitlin. Back again at Joyeux Gard they rode together in the forest or along the riverbank where frogs leaped into the marshy waters like splashing rain. Caitlin and he would sing together in harmony as Dafydd had taught them. He had laughed at how the Scottish Gaels always sang their old pentatonic tunes in unison, and though he knew Irish songs with chiefly solo and perhaps refrain, he liked best the British way of singing always in harmony if they could find more voices than one.

Caitlin sang new songs now from her own country:

Heart is he,
nut of oaks,
brisk one he,
kissed one dotes.

Another she said was sung first by a king's daughter, who ran off with the close comrade – almost a fosterson – of the old chief who wished to marry her:

That fellow –
I tell you thanks, him eyeing;
For him I'd sell earth – yellow,
mellow, all – though bad buying.

Caitlin joined Galahad again in his lessons, and they often read aloud together in British or Latin. At first she gave the women instructions on the clothes she would need for her life in Wales, but later in the summer she let Galahad read to her while she worked away at sewing, weaving, and embroidery, especially at the final touches of decoration.

Galahad managed in secret to copy out a slim volume of hymns as a wedding present, a gift he had carefully illuminated with gold and red and green capitals and vines and scrolls to fill out the lines to an even margin. Hodge made a calfskin cover·for it and sewed the whole together. Galahad placed an Irish cross on the cover, carefully carving it into the leather, and painting it with the bright colors as a glory around it. Caitlin was delighted and carried it with her that first day of August when she was married. The chapel was aglow with new banners and flowers and the sparkle of torches and candles. Caitlin's long red hair was held back in a golden snood. Her blue-green dress was reflected in her blue-green eyes, and her waist was encircled with a flame-colored girdle like her hair, matched by the shoes that peeped out below her dress. Dafydd had come with a new song with the refrain: "the firelight of thy hair." Caitlin had laughed at it, but she could not disguise her delight.

Caitlin's brother rode in from King Mark's court with Tristram and gave the bride away. Elaine was a gracious hostess though in her heart there were tears at all the gladness here that she would never know. No one at all came from Camelot, though Dafydd said he had cousins there, and it was only a day's ride away.

But Joyeux Gard was well named that day and the week following. Then with servants and packhorses, friends and relatives from Wales, the couple rode off northward. Galahad was not to see them again except for a brief visit in later years when he was at last the best knight in the world. He had seen then her happiness with her children about her and the littlest in her arms, the eldest nearly eight. The happiness and love of this household should have made the memory of Joyeux Gard an ache of bleak emptiness, but Galahad found that he or the world had changed by then.

In these years of Galahad's boyhood, England had been maturing too. King Arthur was consolidating his Britain – Logris, it was called – from rival kings, both Welsh and Scottish on the north, and from the Saxons, now pouring in along the flat fenlands of the east. They had come at first after the Roman guards had pulled back to defend the mother city against the marauding barbarians from the Rhine and Danube. Finding a fertile land much like the swamps and islands of the north coast whence they came, the Saxons had happily settled, and now threatened to take over the whole island.

At first Arthur had been much busied in battles and sieges and long marches with his troops. Some of this time Lancelot fought by his side as second in command. At other times he protected one border or commanded one action while Arthur was elsewhere engaged. During these years Guenever and Lancelot had fallen deeper and deeper into the abyss from which it would be so painful to climb.

But the wars had been successful and gradually peace had settled over Logris. The court, except for occasional visits to London, was mainly settled in the southwest. When Saxons actually displaced the British, Winchester became the capital, but for Arthur the capital was west of that, beyond Salisbury but not as far as the Roman town of Ilchester. North of it, not far away was Glastonbury, called then Inis Avalon. There Galahad renewed his vows of baptism with the laying on of hands in that ceremony that had been for him the culmination of that summer.

In the peace that settled on the land, men began to think of their own souls. When the enemy was no longer at the gates, they might strengthen their inner fortress. Now was the great new day at the court of Camelot, and Galahad for the first time had seen a city, had seen a great church, and had felt how temporary his world was.

Chapter IV

Awakening

Goats and Farrows,
wild, tame families
come for food; tall
wild cattle, red deer,
fallow, badgers brood.

Peaceful cluster,
country muster
gathers near;
toward the copses
come the foxes:
lovely here.

Chieftains stunning,
swine come running
crowd about
purest water,
crop for guesting:
salmon, trout.

[from the Irish]

When Galahad was fifteen** he began to have strange experiences. One winter night as he was crossing the courtyard to his chamber he glanced up and saw across the sky a ribbon of light that flickered like flames ascending. Within that curious ring was a strange glow that pulsed with a tinted phosphorescence. Again he heard the sacred choir of angels.

Years ago there had been the calming of the stallion when Galahad prayed. In later years when riding or walking with Caitlin deep in the forest, she sometimes wished for a drink of water. If he breathed a prayer, it seemed that around the next bend they would find a bubbling spring or a splashing brook or a still pool where the hillstream dropped from a ledge into its depths. As he grew older, these experiences multiplied. When he wished, it would rain for the sake of the ploughing or stop raining for haying and harvest; his prayers would within an hour be granted. When a cow or a mare was long in labor, his prayers for the delivery brought quick relief.

But when Galahad was fifteen stranger events occurred. As he was walking by the river one day he paused by the b auk to watch the light sparkling on the water and a water-rat scurrying into a hole on the opposite edge of the stream. A ferret came past him carrying a baby rabbit. In five or ten minutes he saw another, also carrying a baby rabbit. He followed back along their path and saw the parent rabbits guarding each side of the warren and rushing at the first ferret, which had now returned.

Galahad wondered if the ferret too had young, and he began to follow it. This was not easy, but he expected no long chase, considering the time-lapse between visits. It was, however, longer than he had guessed. He would lose sight of the little brown fellow with his erect black-tipped tail, and then as if it were awaiting him, would see it dash across the path, leading him deeper into the woods and farther away from the river. That too seemed strange, for the ferrets had been carrying the rabbits toward the river. But he followed on.

At last he came out of the forest on the edge of a lake, shining in the sunlight. All around was the murmur of a brook over stones, or a little waterfall, or voices – happy voices, chattering together. A great gray heron stalked along the edge of the water and three swans circled near the center. Then it seemed to him the babbling brook or the chorus of voices was calling his name: "Galahad – Galahad – Lancelot du Lac." All he saw there was the heron rise heavily and flap his broad wings until on the other side of the lake he thrust out his long legs and alighted to go on stalking fish and frogs in new hunting grounds. The swans ceased circling and swam off in single file toward the east. But the voices continued: "Lancelot, Lancelot du Lac."

At his left, Galahad noticed a hill rising from beside the lake, and he climbed it for a better view of the lake, and perhaps of the way home. At the top, stones showed through the grasses and a mound of them crowned the summit. Before this, however, and somehow oriented toward the lake was a stone circle. These were familiar all over Devonshire and Somerset, but here the tallest stone had carved on it a cross, a cross with spindle arms and enlarged ends, but clearly a cross. From the circle he could indeed overlook the land, almost to Môr Hafren (the Severn Sea, that is, the Bristol Channel).

The eerie feeling that had possessed him as he stood by the lake gradually dissipated as he turned back toward the river that he knew would form the moat about Joyeux Gard. As he made his way back he pondered: "Why today?" It was the first day of August. On that day three years ago Caitlín had been married. Yes, and she had laughed about the date that had been set: "Lugnasad it'll be then, the feast of Lug, and it's the great god he was, master of many arts – Lug Ildánach. Some say he and not Sualtaim was the father of Cú Chulainn. What a sword he had, like a flashing sunbeam!" Galahad thought of his father's sword "Joyeux" and how the light caught the blade as he swung it.

Autumn had come. The leaves had brightened then faded then fallen. The frosts of winter might come any morning now, and the oak leaves, still clinging red brown to the branches rattled crisply in every breeze. Galahad and the mare enjoyed those days when to keep moving was the best way to keep warm. He had been out with her early in the morning along the river. Now in the forest he found it easier to penetrate the tangle on foot.

As he pushed aside low branches that brushed his face he heard a hawk scream and the next moment, hawk and prey were hurtling through the trees before him onto the leaves that strewed the ground. He rushed toward them, and the accipiter flashed off the through the bare branches. The stockdove lay a moment stunned, then fluttered forward. Wondering how badly hurt she might be, Galahad followed. She kept just ahead of him and he soon realized that she was not seriously injured, but still he kept following and she kept flying only a few yards at a time, keeping just beyond his reach.

In this way he proceeded deeper and deeper into the forest, not noting exactly what course he was taking. Two hours later they reached a little clearing. An old man was just entering it with a basket of hazelnuts when the dove fluttered in and perched on his arm. "Well, my dear," he said, "long away you've been, and you ruffled and weary." At the idiom, Galahad thought of Caitlin. The hermit had a strange tonsure that ran over the top of the head from ear to ear, leaving an odd tuft in front and broadened toward the back by the natural balding of age.

Looking up from the bird, the little brown figure turned to Galahad. "It is good with me

your coming," he said. "Will you be in hunger
or thirst? It is only water I can offer, or milk in
a little."

Galahad asked for water and the hermit
dipped him a cupful from the spring that
bubbled out under a rock nearby. At the farther edge of the clearing stood a hut, sheltered
by an ash and a hazel. A large oaktree stood
behind, shading the oratory completely, and a
table with the steeply sloped surfaces of a
scriptorium stood in front with quills ready cut,
a pot of ink, a small piece of split deerskin for a
wiper, and a book that apparently was ready to
copy.

"It is here I'm at working. Dark it is inside, but a fine place there for praying. Would
it be good with you praying now? I'm seeing by
the sun it is time."

Galahad swallowed the water, and bend-
ing almost double followed the little man inside.
A shrine with a single taper before it gave a little
light, and the two knelt side by side at their
prayers, the hermit with an unfamiliar pronunciation of the Latin.

When they emerged again in the last flick-
ers of sunlight, Galahad inquired whether the
hermit was tired of Ireland and how he happened to be here in England. The hermit chuckled.

"I'm knowing all about you, Galahad," he
said, "it is fitting your knowing of me. Donnán,
the little brown one, is the name that I've put
on me. It is brown my robe, and brown my eye,

and brown the bit of hair is left me." He ran a hand over his head. The hair was quite gray, and Galahad guessed he had been long without a mirror. He continued: "It is from Ireland I'm after coming. There do be hermits galore crowding the place. If it is a lonely spot to be seeking, then it is out of Ireland it is proper to come. In Ciarraige there is a mass of wee huts all within the cast of a stone of one another. I set out in my currach, and the winds and waves and currents brought me to Cornwall. From there I came here for the quiet of it. I have my dove and my deer; the wild beasts all come to me for food. Indeed, I must spread some now, for hunger will be taking them with the twilight."

Donnán proceeded to empty the basket of nuts, broken pieces of bread, the bones and entrails of fish on a flat stone at the edge of the clearing. Presently Galahad heard rustling, saw a stirring of the bracken, and squirrels, rabbits, birds and deer crowded about. Then a bit later they suddenly disappeared and a fox and a wild pig came.

"You will share my hut tonight?" Donnán asked. "I shall put you on the road tomorrow, but there is much I would be saying to you."

Galahad again had the feeling that his life was all planned for him, and that he was somehow being kept uninformed. Perhaps this hermit could help him. It grew chill with the setting of the sun. The hermit pulled some loaves from an outside oven. They were nicely browned and that fresh warm smell reminded

Galahad of how little he had eaten all day. Donnán then proceeded to make porridge over a fire, started with the embers raked from below the oven. To this he added chopped toasted hazel nuts, that had been set at the outer edge of the oven and dried berries from a little depression at the top. Though the mixture had no meat at all and not much salt, it tasted very good indeed. They ate from a bowl with plenty of milk. It was deer's milk, Donnán told him and added, "Glad they are to give it when I feed them so well, and the little ones fall to the wolves."

Warmed by the meal they withdrew to the oratory and its one taper. Sheltered from the wind in that small wattled hut covered with turf, they found it pleasantly friendly and comfortable.

"You apeak Latin, of course," said Donnán in that language. Galahad noticed that the hermit spoke it fluently and much more readily than he spoke British, though his pronunciation differed from Galahad' s. Brito-Latin was based more exclusively on the Latin of the soldiers that had been encamped there so long.

"I have questions," said Galahad, "that have long troubled me. Perhaps you could help me to answers."

"That is why I am here," Donnán replied.

"Perhaps it is arrogance on my part to think this is so," began the boy, "but it has seemed to me that my little prayers were quickly answered."

"What kind of 'little prayers' – how little?"

Galahad told of stilling the horse when he was three and of later occasions when riding with Caitlín.

"It is clear," said Donnán, "that always you were praying for someone or something else, never for yourself. That is the way to God's heart."

"But," broke in the boy, "my big prayers for others have never been answered."

"What sort of prayers and for whom?"

"More than for anything else, I have prayed for the happiness of my father and mother, but I have never seen either one happy, except perhaps my mother at her prayers, and then it seems merely the absence of pain."

"My boy, you know, of course, about your parents?"

Galahad nodded. He had heard the gossip of the servants.

"Your mother twice deceived your father. He had no desire for her at all."

"But it was destined I should be born of those two. Everyone admitted that."

"Yes, your mother had had a miserable life before then. She deserved that, and after all it was King Pelles and Dame Brisen who set the trap. That may have been forgivable. But trap him the same way a second time so that he went mad – five years of his life wasted in madness and despair – it is hard to foresee the end of penance for that. Keep up your prayers for them. They do you more good than they do her now, but she has indeed spent a life of suffering in this world, and God will not deny her the peace of heaven in the next."

"And my father?"

"He longs for and prays for something that is contrary to the laws of heaven or earth. He knows that, and he deeply admires King Arthur. Every day of his life is a torment, but his feelings of guilt do not prevent his seizing those moments of joy that may be offered. He has so much goodness in him that he, too, will conquer himself, and will find heaven – not directly as a saint as Elaine will, but after a chastening in Purgatory. Meanwhile he must learn to see himself in a broader perspective, and to that end, his stolen happiness is a hindrance.

"You, my boy, are to be the only knight of purity and virtue as well as might in battle. Keep as unselfish and loving as you are. Worldly joy is never to be yours, and like Cú Chulainn, you will die young, before your father learns repentance."

The boy asked then about that recent afternoon when he had followed the ferret. He asked about the ring of standing stones, the cross, the lake, and the voices. He could almost hear them now: "Galahad – Galahad – Lancelot du Lac."

"There is no escaping the past," said the hermit. "We all come from pagans and sunworshipers like those that raised the stones. But your way is toward Christ as that stone with a cross pointed to you. It pointed to the east, did it not?"

In the darkness, the boy murmured agreement and Donnán continued: "Your father, thanks to the Lady of the Lake, was close to magic. She has not forgotten that you are his son. But you have heard voices elsewhere, have you not?" Again the boy admitted it and Donnán added quietly: "You are much loved of God. He watches you every hour. If you listen to His whispers, you will ever grow closer to Him."

Now the hermit dropped Latin for his Irish-British. "There's a laugh in the merry eye of a maid that promises warmth and comfort, and there is love and laughter in the eye of God that is the deepest warmth and comfort. The one – it's you will never be holding of it in the darkness; the other will always be yours, day and night, in sun and storm, without change, without fail. Remember in so far as it is better you are than others, it is only luckier you are. Never forget laughter, either, when it is kind and loving, like God's own smiles."

The candle light by now had dwindled, guttered, and was gone. "It will be All Hallows' Day the morn," added the hermit. "They call it Samhain in Ireland as you British call it the first of winter. The old gods will be at coming from the hills and barrows. It is from the barrows the name Sid is on them. Sleep well. I'll put you on the road by dawn."

Man and boy rolled in the blankets they had been sitting on and slept. This night Galahad dreamed of entering heaven and finding his mother there before him, radiant and smiling. Together they had turned back to look down through an opening in the clouds to earth. His father was riding back from a tournament toward Camelot. In the way of dreams, Galahad knew every blow struck in the tournament and every rider toppled. He knew, too, the glow of anticipation in Lancelot's heart as he headed toward Guenever. Elaine had laughed happily as she watched him: "He will come to us, my son, in his own time, but it is a long, long road for him until then. God bless him and guide him – and God bless her, too." The boy felt the warmth and peace of all that endless world, and sighed happily in his sleep.

On his way home next day Galahad thought over what he had learned. God does indeed answer our prayers, if they do not run counter to His plan. One can, then, pray for great things or small, for it puts no compulsion on God. He grants His children what they need, withholds what may harm their souls. He is merciful; He may be trusted. If one is unlucky, he may sin, but God will not desert even him, if he admit his fault, repent, and ask forgivenness. The punishment may be severe, but never more than a man can bear, and the heavenly prize at last will be worth all the pain to win it.

Then he thought of himself. Donnán had called him luckier than others, not better than they. "Could he mean that I can learn to avoid sin by seeing the consequences to others?" Galahad wondered. "Will I be lucky in never being tempted? Perhaps I am more of a coward than my father who dared to sin." The thought was humbling and he regarded Lancelot in a new way, but he also thought, "Yet perhaps he is more of a fool than I." Elaine would have agreed with this. The only solution was love and trust in God, Who would betray no one.

In firmer faith than ever and with still more joy in that belief, Galahad made his way home by following the brook that began in the spring by the hermitage and ran into the river past Joyeux Gard. Running through his head were the songs Donnán had sung as he stirred the porridge, tended the fire, or set out food for the wild creatures. Some of them he had already learned from Caitlin, songs full of the love of the earth and praise of its beauty. He hummed some of them as he walked back through the woods.

Overwatch'd by woodland wall,
merles make melody full well;
above my book – lined, lettered –
birds twittered a soothing spell.
Cuckoos call clear – fairest phrase –
cloaked in grays,from leafy leas;
Lord's love, what blessings show'ring.
Good to write 'neath tow'ring trees.

And then:

Starry King,
black or white my house within,

closed to none its doors shall be,
lest Christ close to me His inn.

But most haunting was the one Donnán had sung in his sweet Irish tenor voice just before his last prayers of the evening:

Be it sundown, be it dawn,
land or ocean be it on,
my death will come – this I know –
the hour – woe – unknown till gone.

That adventure was not easily forgotten. For many a year thereafter when someone called him the best knight in the world, he would shake his head and say no, only the luckiest. Luckiest – happiest – richest – most blessed – most gifted – these were all the same. All were gifts of God, not of long endeavor.

But there remained another lesson to learn before Galahad was ready to set out for Camelot and knighthood. At seventeen that adventure crossed his path. He had ridden down along the river and then crossed over the downs where the red deer moved in restless herds, past stone circles and monoliths, these latter standing against the sky so that from one, the next crowned the following rise, marking the way from a refuge of monks in south Devon all the way to Camelot and on to Glastonbury. The sun was warm and all about the larks were leaping skyward, bounding up an invisible stair and a torrent of song gushing from each fluttering speck as it rose.

Galahad dismounted in the shelter of a rocky tor and let Kate graze beside him. The lulling of birdsongs, the warmth of the sun, the luxury of this first perfect day of spring brought first drowsiness and at last sleep. On that day Galahad had been reminded of a tale of Cú Chulainn that Caitlin had once told him. She said it was the only jealousy of Emir, Cú Chulainn's wife. Since he had been thinking of that, it is not surprising that he dreamed of it, of lying in a field with larks all about and two women beating him in turn. Perhaps half an hour, perhaps an hour later Kate whinnied and Galahad opened his eyes. He was deep in the dream – an unpleasant one-with a feeling of somehow having done amiss, of having displeased someone who deserved kindness. Then he realized that someone was looking at him and he sat up.

She was sitting on a rock, a smile in those bright blue eyes, the iris dark at the rim, dark curling lashes above and below, smoothly arching eyebrows and cheeks of a natural brightness. Soft dark redbrown hair curled over her forehead and hung almost to her waist, like a young girl's. Her dress was the blue of her eyes, and a dark mantle lined with flame, its cowl thrown back~covered her shoulders.

"You must be Galahad," she said. The red mouth showed the tips of small even teeth as she smiled at him.

"Yes," he admitted. "Have you been here long?"

"Long enough, perhaps twenty minutes."

"How do you know who I am?"

Galahad lived a lonely life, seeing little of the village, indeed, only the two or three encouraged to come to Joyeux Gard to practice swordsmanship and tilting could he call by name.

"I'm living not far away," she replied. My family –" she corrected herself, "my mother's family are from Cornwall, but even where I come from, we have heard of your father. He is the best knight of the world, is he not?"

"It is said so," Galahad answered, slightly embarrassed.

"We are all in love with him," persisted the girl. "Of course there is Sir Tristram, too. But it is said Lancelot has eyes only for the Queen. Such devotion! Any one of us would give the world for such a man."

Galahad recalled Caitlin's song:

That fellow –
I tell you thanks, him eyeing;
For him I'd give earth yellow,
Mellow, all – though bad buying.

He blushed in annoyance and said stiffly: "My father is not here; he rarely comes here."

"But you are his son and nearer our age," she insisted.

"Who are the others?" he asked, trying

to turn the talk away from his family.

"My sisters, my cousins, my people. We live beyond that coombe. It is only a few miles from Castle Bliant and Joyeux Gard."

"It is strange we never met before," he said, actually not eager to meet her again, perhaps because he was aware of her loveliness and of the strange attraction as if he were still dreaming and she was part of that dream.

"We never met because I have been away – across the sea. But now I am here for a while."

"You come from Ireland?~' he asked. "Your speech is not Irish."

"No, I come from Man," she said. "Surely you've heard of it."

"Yes," said he. "You understand Irish then."

"A little, a little, but I think of myself as Cornish."

"Since you already know my name, may I ask yours?"

"Oh, how thoughtless of me. They call me Keren," she laughed like the tinkle of a silver bell. "That is Cornish for darling or little love." Galahad felt uneasy, but her disarming laughter was a caution not to take her seriously.

"Now while you were sleeping," she continued, "I wove you this coronet of flowers. If you had slept two minutes longer, you would have waked crowned with it. Here take it."

Galahad took the wreath and looked at it, but he did not put it on.

"Your mare almost ate it," she laughed.

"It is just as well she didn't," he said quietly. "You have made it of nightshade, hyssop,
and mandrake. In what witches garden did you
find these?"

Keren's eyes were wide in surprise. "I did
not know. How dreadful it would have been,"
she exclaimed. Snatching it from him, she tore
it to bits, her cheeks hot with annoyance.

"No harm has been done," he laughed.
Up until now he had felt she had the advantage
of him – coming on him asleep, intruding into
his dream. Now he was more relaxed, and since
his acceptance of the wreath had been so un-
gracious, he tried to be friendly.

"Let us walk down the hill, then," he suggested. "There is blackthorn in bloom there."

He led the mare with one hand and took
Keren's arm to help her, for the way was rough.
She was tiny and slim, scarcely to his shoulder, though he was yet half a head shorter than
Lancelot. She stooped gracefully to lift her skirt
a bit to make the walking easier. Dainty as she
was, the curve of her breasts, the grace of her
step, her little mouth and the large, wide-apart
eyes made Galahad think that neither Caitlin
nor his mother were so delightfully propor-
tioned.

When he had broken for her sprays of
the foam-white blossoms and seen them crowning her dark hair and heard her gasp of delight
and rippling laughter, he thought her quite the
loveliest of women.

She would not let him go home with her,

insisting it was really quite nearby, and so they parted by the river, the mare restive to return and Keren's little figure standing straight and still by the water's edge until he was out of sight.

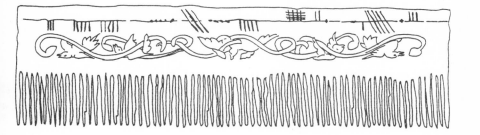

Chapter V

Man

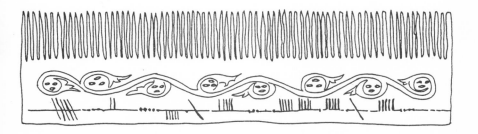

mountain snow, white the hollow
wild winds twist trees and bellow:
many pairs feel love's arrow,
but never meet their fellow.

mountain snow, the stag away,
heart laughs on its love today;
though one tell me a story,
I saw the shame where it lay.

mountain snow, they hunt the hart,
winds whined on high rampart:
sin hangs heavy on the heart.

mountain snow, flecked front of rock,
reeds rough, beasts restless flock:
woe to him whose wife men mock.

[from the Welsh]

The next day an ouzel outside wakened Galahad at dawn. Running in and out of his dreams had been the thought of Keren mixed with that tale of Cú Chulainn. But Cú had lain helpless for a year, and had sent his charioteer off to fairyland. Galahad remembered much of the story, but he could not remember the end. He shrugged. He was clearly not Cú Chulainn: no wife, no charioteer, and she a lone girl walking on the moors. Yet only in Irish stories were girls walking out alone, and those were always from the Sid or Tir na n-Óg or the Land under Waves.

That afternoon again Galahad set off to the northwest. As he mounted the hill toward the tor, there she sat on a low rock, humming to herself and plaiting reeds into a basket. So, thought he, she must have come from a river or a lake. He thought of the voices by the lake that other day two or more years ago. Keren's voice was low and a sense of enchantment, a mystery beyond that of other women enveloped her.

She looked up at his approach. Her smile was glad, her blue, blue eyes, bright in the shadow of those dark lashes, sparkled, and her cheeks glowed like the petals of the wild rose. Galahad had left the mare among the sallows at the foot of the hill, and now he sat down beside Keren, quietly smoothing out the reeds she had gathered as her deft fingers wove the others quickly and neatly.

As they talked, he learned that her family – or her mother's family – had lands at the eastern border of Cornwall. Apparently mines and clay pits had been the source of highly successful enterprises and her father, it would seem, transported the produce as a ship owner from the Isle of Man. All this was vague with many assumptions on his part to fill gaps in the story. Two points were clear: it was unlikely that she came of a family of rank, though it must have been a wealthy one, for her clothes – today a blue dress again with coral silk girdle, pink coral necklace, and a coral lining to her soft brown cape and hood – were of excellent quality. The other point he was sure of: Dame Brisen and his mother would not approve.

The basket Keren wove was not large. It was like a fisherman's creel, but oval, and she had used broad rushes for the basic frame with slender reeds interwoven and split stems of willow for rim and handle. When it was done, he walked with her as she gathered tender herbs just sprouting in this first spring warmth, and mushrooms from the edges of the marshy ground where she had gathered the reeds. All the frogs and insects were suddenly silent as they approached. He remembered, too, that no larks had been singing the day before after he awoke.

Again she would not let him follow her. "My horse is in the glade by the lake," she said. He followed her, and indeed, there was the horse and there the lake he had seen before with the babbling brook running from it toward the river.

He heard its muttering, "Warily, warily, Galahad du Lac"·

"Do you see many ferrets here?" he asked.

"Hardly," she laughed. "They are very shy and there are not many of them."

Galahad held the stirrup while she mounted the little chestnut, hardly bigger than his moor pony of so many years ago. Its coat was just the color of Keren's hair and its creamy mane was pale as her little hands on the reins. "Tomorrow?" he asked without meaning to. She answered with a slow smile as she looked down into his blue-gray eyes.

On the third day he set out earlier. The larks were again all about. He walked around the tor and found again the stone circle with the crude cross on the stone pointing eastward. The chattering stream fell splashing from the lake murmuring: "Galahad – Galahad – Galahad watch out!" Of course the babbling would say anything that was in one's mind already, and only after listening a while could he hear anything intelligible.

At that moment the chestnut pony and the dainty rider appeared. He no longer heard the voices in the brook nor the larks in the clouds, but after all, he was no longer listening for them. Keren's low voice always made her conversation seem intimate and mysterious. He wondered how old she was. Tiny as she was, she seemed young. He would have guessed her to be younger than he, but she had an assurance, a sense of having made clear only just so much as she wanted made clear that he thought it likely that she was older – a year or two perhaps.

As she slipped off the pony into his arms, she let her hands rest on his shoulders a moment, her eyes looking up into his, her lips parted in a gentle smile, showing just the tips of those small white teeth. Galahad was surprised at what he felt. Nothing of the kind had ever touched him before. Caitlin had always treated him as an equal, but they had both avoided personal contact. She was considerably taller than the little boy of twelve who admired her, and she was kind enough not to patronize him. Though he adored her, he had never felt that she saw in him anything but a companion who relieved the boredom of joyless Joyeux Gard.

Galahad's heart was pounding, but Keren held him only a moment, and slipped away almost as soon as he released her. "You came early," was all she said, but her low voice thrilled through him.

He rushed into conversation to cover his confusion even from himself. "I came here once before, years ago. I hadn't seen it again since." He looked out across the lake and a small wild swan, perhaps injured and unable to leave for the breeding, called "Who? Who?" and swam into the thick reeds lining the lake.

Keren was laughing. "Yesterday and the day before we sat just the other side of the tor."

But he plunged on. "My father is Lancelot

du Lac. I always wondered if this could be his lake. There was a Lady of the Lake who used to visit him now and then." He paused. Keren was looking down but flashed him a quick glance. She said nothing. They moved in silence away from the lake and a bluegreen kingfisher darted past them with its sharp call.

Swallows were skimming the other side of the tor as they walked on toward the wood at its foot. The wood stretched from the river across a broad band of rugged hills almost to the edge of the Severn Sea. A huge old oak at the edge stretched wide arms above a well. Keren paused and tossed in a coin. "For good luck," she said. They watched the circles grow to the edge and then blur as they met the returning circle. A frog croaked.

"Are you going into the woods?" she asked, turning to him.

"Yes, I thought it a pleasant way we haven't yet gone."

She said no more, but after they moved beyond the sheltering branches of the oak, she pressed closer to him and took his hand. He felt his heart leap within him. "Does the forest trouble you?" he asked. "We needn't walk here."

For answer she held his hand tighter and he felt the curve of her breast on the back of his wrist. "How beautiful it is here," she exclaimed.

Some large animal – stag? boar? wolf? – went crashing away through the underbrush. They could see only the swaying thicket and heard the call of a raven in the tree tops. Now she crowded yet closer under his protecting arm, her shoulder close to his heart. And yet it flashed through his mind that she was not frightened but merely taking advantage of the enclosing branches. At once he dismissed the thought as unworthy of him or her. He had no reason at all to think her deceitful. Reticent, yes, talking more of him than of herself, but frank and friendly.

He spoke soothingly, "There is no danger here, but perhaps we should go back to the hills. The great clouds are piling up today and we miss all that grandeur in here." She was still holding his hand and gazing up at him, but she followed meekly, and as they stepped out from the thorn trees at the forest edge, she let him withdraw his hand.

That evening he prayed longer than usual, and for the next three days he did not turn in that direction. He tried instead to find his way back to the hermitage where he had spent a night with Donnán a couple of years before. He found it on the third day, but it was deserted. Only a few empty nutshells, a dish that might have contained milk for some young creature showed that this was the place. The cross inside was gone and the altar overturned. It must have lain in disuse for at least a year, perhaps longer, for the cress in the spring outside was growing lush. Galahad nibbled at a handful of it as he walked away, strangely disappointed and keenly aware of the stillness now

– no murmur of wooddoves or flutter of wings, no rustlings in the thicket, nor grunting of wild hogs.

On the seventh day since first meeting Keren, Galahad again returned to the lake, this time on foot. As he approached the tor he saw her sitting there, combing the chestnut waves of her hair. She looked up with her gentle smile that showed just the tips of her white teeth, and she tossed back the soft curls. Nothing in her greeting seemed warmer or colder than before.

"I was looking for an old friend these last days," he said, feeling some explanation of his absence was due.

"Oh, really?" she replied. "All sorts of matters kept me away. I hadn't noticed."

He wondered if she were telling the truth, but she certainly had showed no unusual pleasure at seeing him, nor had she pouted and seemed distant. He wondered, but he did not comment. On an impulse he touched the hair that tumbled over her shoulders. It was finer than Caitlin's, curlier too. His mother hid hers under her headdress. He had sometimes wondered if she had cut it off like a nun's. Keren offered him the comb. "You may comb it if you like. It is in such a tangle."

There on the sunny side of the tor he ran the comb through those rich, fragrant tresses. They smelled of lavender and pine needles, of mint from the shallows and new-mown grasses. She closed her eyes as he combed as if falling under enchantment. He paused in the combing, and she laid her head back on his knee, looking up at him. But he was studying the comb.

Scrolls and leaf-patterns twisting together were carved above the teeth, but the spine of it had no marks except a series of irregular scratches, some running over the edge, some merely notches. Most, however, ran down toward the teeth. He had never before seen bone so white.

"Do you like my comb?" she asked.

"Yes, it is most unusual."

"Along the back it has my name."

"In what writing?"

"That is ogam. Surely you have heard of that."

He examined it. "Yes, Cú Chulainn used to put ogam on sticks and then none might pass that way. But I had never seen it," he added.

"This side has my name," she said, pointing it out. "An Irishman carved it from the tooth of some seamonster and it was given to me."

"What does it say on the other side?" he asked.

She laughed mischievously. "That's the magic," she said and would say no more.

After this day Galahad began leaving for the tor in the morning, bringing cheese from the dairy and bread from the oven for his lunch. With watercress, which grew abundantly in the talkative brook that flowed from the lake, he had a pleasant lunch and Keren was always there before him with a basket of similar fare.

They never talked of whether they would come early or late, but they always met.

One afternoon Galahad found himself humming a tune of Caitlin's that he had especially liked. Dafydd had said it was good enough to be Welsh and the three had often sung it together. Since then, however, his voice had begun to go out of control and he sang little. But now Keren joined in with the words. Her voice was low and of little power, a contrast to Caitlin's brilliance in music, but the softness of her speech and song always made her talk, and now her singing, seem personal, intimate. Galahad, careful to keep his voice under control sang softly too:

Summer's come, safe, sound,
it bound the black brake;
leaping deer, spry, slim;
seals swim with smooth wake.

Cuckoos call – choir sweet –
as we sleep, dream, drift;
past calm coombs birds dart;
hart is hoar, swift.

Heat seized den of deer;
"Good cheer!" howled the hound;
sea smiled on bleached beach
where each wild wave wound.

Blind wind whined on mound,
oaks round Drum Dell dim;

great groomed stallions bolt
in Cuan Holt shut in.

Green bursts on all herb tops,
green oak copse of great trees;
hinds hurt by holly run;
summer's come, winter flees.

Theirs the wounding wood,
merles good music sing;
strong sad seas asleep,
flecked fish leap and spring.

For me storm leaves its stand
each land smiles the sun:
daws will thrive, a dog barks,
harts will herd – summer's come!

The five-syllable lines, the galloping monosyllables, the constant echoes within lines as well as the end-rhymes set them laughing as they had sung ever faster with Galahad's growing confidence in his voice. After that Galahad began to bring his harp. Keren taught him Cornish and Manx ballads, but perhaps because her voice had not the quality of Caitlın's, he preferred the Irish songs of his boyhood.

The meetings with Keren were like the tales of encounters with women of the sid who seemed always to be awaiting the kings of Ireland. Perhaps that was why a few days later Galahad sang Midir's song, summoning Etain to fairyland.

Woman fair, to lands aglow
with magic stars wilt thou go?
Like primrose petals is the hair,
and bodies there are like snow.

There is neither mine nor thine;
brows are black there, bright teeth shine;
fair to see our hosts are spread;
each cheek there glows foxglove red.

Purple plain is every moor;
fair to see are merles' eggs pure;
Eire was a lovely sight –
lonely, since Great Plain's delight.

Though heady seems Ireland's beer,
more heady the Great Land's here;
grand the land of which I told:
young die not before the old.

Sweet streams flow for earth, and then,
choice mead and wine there for men;
fine perfect people there breathe,
sinless, guiltless they conceive.

Everyone we see each way
and none sees us: dark of day
from sin of Adam mounting
hides us from any counting.

Woman, if thou come with me,
crown of gold we'll give to thee;

fresh pork, ale, and milk prepare
as shine with me, woman fair.

Galahad sang this alone and then she replied with another. The song was from that story of Cú Chulainn that had been in his head as he slept on the hillside the first day Keren appeared. He felt vaguely uneasy, though he knew the songs well. He leaned on an elbow in the grass, listen-ing as she sang Fand's greet-ing to Cú Chu-lainn.

Arise, O Ulster's fighter!
Wake from sleep bolder, brighter!
See their king, daybreak peeping;
give yourself no longsleeping.

See his shoulder crystal clear;
see his flagons with fine beer;
see his chariots charge the glen;
see his ranks drawn like chessmen.

See his comrades strong of limb;
see his maidens tall and slim;
see his kings, their course daring;
see his queens all charm bearing.

See bright winter nearer come;
see each wonder, one by one;
see by thee what serves thee more
its cold, its length, its palor.

Deep sleep is waste, dead and dull,

faint from fight unequal;
drink when sated is long rest;
weaker than all, death weakest.

Rouse from sleep, though drink brings peace;
strike at violent furies.
Soft speech sought love to aver:
Arise, O Ulster's fighter!

Keren's voice sank almost to a whisper on the last two lines and she slowly raised her long dark lashes to gaze full at the boy as she finished. He realized too late that he might have prevented the embarrassment by singing with her. Just then a merlin came hurtling from the sky and pounced on a dunnock that was hunting nesting materials near them. Galahad jumped to his feet and frightened the predator off, fortunately for the dunnock, that had been rolled over but not seriously hurt. He came back grinning. "That was a narrow escape!" he said.

Her face was turned from him, but she glanced quickly over her shoulder at him. "Indeed it was," ended their conversation.

After Mayday new flowers seemed to have bloomed each morning, and they used

to meet with a fresh bouquet. Who had found the freshest, the earliest, the handsomest? Then followed haying and sheepshearing. By July the hills were covered with berries. Cranberries in the bogs, bilberries and whortles on the slopes. It seemed to rain only at night and every day was sunny by noon. All the plants flourished and yet day after day they could walk on the downs. Galahad wondered about this glorious and unfamiliar weather only to rejoice in it and to rejoice at his daily visits with Keren.

The turbulence she could arouse in him, however, made him set certain limits. He tried not to be present when she dismounted from the chestnut pony. He did not wander with her into the woods, except along the river's edge where the ground was damp and rocky – uninviting.

It was late in July when she said to him one day, her fingertips and her lips blue with the berries she had been eating "In all this summer we've made little progress in friendship, don't you think?"

"We see a good bit of each other," he answered. "You have not let me go with you, and my home is an empty shell where you would find little pleasure."

"But I didn't mean we needed to expand our friendship that way," she said. She refused to be more explicit, and soon went to wash the berry stains from her fingers.

Down at the edge of the lake where she dipped her hands she found something struggling in the grass. She came running back to Galahad with a baby rabbit that had been caught in a snare by one leg. She sat down by him, cradling the little soft one in her lap trying to disentangle the tough strands of horsehair that had been used. "It couldn't have been meant for a rabbit, perhaps for moles or shrews," he suggested, kneeling before her. "All it could catch was a baby."

At last the hairs were unwound, but the muscles were strained so the foot dragged and they bent over it together to be sure the leg was not dislocated. At the same moment they decided that the damage was not serious and raised their heads. Her lips were two inches from his and the fragrance of her hair brushed his cheek. He was never sure afterwards which one kissed the other, but suddenly her lips were pressed to his and her tongue softly tasted his lips. She sank back, pulling him toward her as the rabbit, still limping, hopped away.

At that moment came a deafening thunderclap and her hair rose all about her in a glory. A black cloud was rapidly covering the sky from the direction of the tor behind them. Flashes of lightning and angry rumblings sent them scrambling for their horses, and hardly looking at each other they mounted and rode off in opposite directions.

The storm that drenched them before they reached home heralded a week of savage winds and drenching downpours. Galahad, whose reading had been confined to the long hours of summer twilight, now plunged into his studies with fresh enthusiasm. He recognized that he was glad of the storm, ashamed of his lack of control, embarrassed at the thought of seeing Keren again, and content to try to think the matter through.

At the end of the week he had come to a
conclusion. Why should he not marry her?
Other knights married; Cú Chulainn was married; if his father had married his mother and
had paid her the same devotion he paid the
queen, there might have been gladness in
Joyeux Gard. He would ask his mother and the
priest, but first he must ask Keren.

The end of the week was the first day of
August. Galahad smiled as he thought of all the
adventures that had happened to him on
Lugnasad, and when the day dawned clear with
only a light mist that burned away by
midmorning, he felt that this was to be his lucky
day. He whistled as he saddled the mare, and
she too seemed eager to stir out again and
nuzzled him as he passed.

Keren was seated this time near the stone
circle and jumped to her feet as she heard his
step. He could read the delight in her eyes, and
she threw her arms about him as he drew her
toward him. The softness of her lips, the curve
of her breasts against him sent a delicious shiver
through him and he half expected a thunderclap.

Instead a deep voice said, "Well, my dear,
I see I need not have worried about your loneliness while I was at sea."

Galahad and Keren sprang apart and he
turned to see a tall, heavyset man with grizzled
hair and beard. The stranger had come up behind Galahad, and since Galahad, already a
head taller than Keren, had grown two inches

since Easter, she could not see beyond him. But now she stepped over to the stranger's side and took his hand. Her voice was dead and cold.

"Galahad, this is my husband, Mannan Mac Lir."

"If I surprise you," said Mannan with a touch of irony, "I landed here one afternoon about a week ago. I planned to take my wife back from her parents at once, but weather prevented."

Neither Galahad nor Keren said a word or looked at each other. Mannan continued jocularly. "You can scarcely be surprised. Haven't you seen her walrus comb with both our names on it? Of course that crazy Irish gobae used his own forms of the names. I gave the comb to Fannin at our wedding." Still the two said nothing, and Mannan continued.

"My wife always finds ways to keep life interesting. As you may gather, she finds young boys more refreshing than a man like me, but never fear, we have good fun together for all that. It is the adventure, the excitement to see if she can indeed stir the heart of the young that leads her to play this game. You are not the first, and" – he sighed – "you will not be the last. Come Fannin."

She turned and followed him, never raising her eyes. Galahad saw her grasp Mannan's hand and kiss it just as they were almost out of sight.

Galahad rode back home humiliated and angry. He saw why his father would never marry

Elaine. No man can bear to be made a fool of. Keren – so she had called herself, but Mannan had called her Fannín – Keren had deceived him: she wanted him to think her mother was of Cornwall, but it was her husband, not her father whom she had followed to Man. And how old was she? Not the first. She had undertaken to deceive him with her flowing hair like a maiden's, the limits she set to what she communicated. He should have been warned by that wreath of poisonous weeds on their first meeting. Wounded vanity is the grave of love, and for Galahad the bitterness of this experience so reinforced his earlier impressions of the relations between men and women that from then on he could not be at ease in a woman's company.

At last, too, he remembered what the hermit had said: he would never hold the warmth and comfort of a woman in the darkness. "And I shall never know what it is to lose it," he thought. He prayed deep into the night, at first asking God's forgiveness, and then as he felt the humiliation of the afternoon dwindle and withdraw he prayed in gratitude for the peace and love of God that wrapped him round.

Galahad fell asleep long after midnight. It was a restless sleep. As on the day of first meeting, Keren had seemed to be part of a dream of that tale of Cú Chulainn that Caitlín used to tell. He dreamed of the parting when Fand renounces Cú Chulainn to go with her husband, Manannan Mac Lir – a great shadowy god-like

figure, less clear, more grand than **Mannan.**
What haunted him was the memory of **Fand's**
farewell song that **Keren** sang to him, not in
her own low, husky voice but in **Caitlin's high,**
thrilling tones.

See the warrior son of Lir
from plains of Eogan Inbir:
Manannan mounts the world's hill;
his love once my heart would fill.

Today my cry would be sharp;
no love lies in heavy heart;
for love is a vain affair,
quickly fading everywhere.

I found it fitting and just
for women are not to trust:
he whom I loved beyond all
has brought about my downfall.

Farewell kind Cú, here abide;
I go from thee in high pride.
Parting wish is left undone:
good every rule till broken.

It is time for me to go;
one finds it hard – that I know.
Great indeed the loss I fear,
O Loeg son of Riangabir.

I shall go with my own mate:
he breaks not my will, my fate.

Do not say in stealth I flee.
Watch if you will; let all see.

Galahad waked, the dream clearer to him than
the reality of the morning light falling across
the floor. But as he dressed he realized that
Keren had felt no such pain at parting as had
Fand. He breathed a long sigh and felt once more
the peace and serenity and comfort of God's loving care.

Chapter VI

The Best Knight
in the World

I have set my hert so hye,
Me liketh no love that lowere is;
And alle the paines that I may drye,
Me think it do me good, y-wis.

For on that Lorde that loved us alle
So hertely have I set my thought,
It is my joye on Him to calle.
For love me hath in bales brought,
Me think it do me good, y-wis.

Middle English lyric

hen Galahad took his leave of Elaine and of the priest who had taught him so much, he was eighteen. He had said his farewells to the servants the night before. The cook had been in tears and the groom had said tersely, "We'll miss 'e lad." Kate had nuzzled him and slobbered on his jacket and the hounds had wagged their tails, looking up with great brown eyes and shaggy muzzles in perplexity.

He was eighteen and he thought himself a greater fool and a greater coward than most. He had been duped by the first girl who had looked soulfully at him. He was afraid of, or at least strongly disliked, violence and pain, especially when others must suffer. He felt his chief virtues were sincerity and a love for God that he felt with all his heart, that gave him comfort in darkness and trouble, and a feeling of radiance and peace at every hour of the day, especially in the still moments when God seemed very close.

The priest and his mother, he knew, thought him a fine fellow, but they knew only a small part of his thoughts and that was the best part. He knelt now before them to ask their blessing. The priest pronounced it with fervor, then Elaine held out both her hands and raised him to his feet. He was as tall as his father now, and as he looked down into her eyes – so like his father all those years ago – she sighed deeply but smiled in true happiness.

"My son," she said, "this castle is yours

when you wish. I have nothing more to keep me here, and I shall withdraw from the world. Bless you for restoring my faith that men can be both great and good. If I have not showed you the tenderness you might have wished, neither have I smothered you with my hopes and heartache. And yet you have fulfilled the highest wishes a mother might have for her son. As my last request, let it be your father who gives you knighthood. He owes you that."

He answered, adopting her tone which was neither tearful nor sentimental: "Mother, I already owe him much, for he taught me manliness and the importance of skill at arms. I shall be honored if he will do me also this favor."

"Bless you, then," said she, "and may God keep you both." She lifted her face to him and he bent and kissed her on the brow.

The priest, a round little man no taller than Elaine, stepped forward now, making the sign of the cross. "Son, you have been a diligent pupil. May it profit you always. Please accept this remembrance in memory of us all." He fumbled under his robe and produced a missal, two palms' breadth tall and a palm wide. It was newly copied, and one could see the love and care that had gone into it. From Father Peter, Galahad had learned a careful script, but he never achieved the graceful perfection of illumination of his teacher.

"Father," he said with a smile, "this missal is a treasure and a delight. It will be a daily reminder of you and of all you have taught me."

"But you go a different road now," the priest reminded him. "Horses, swords, and armor will be your daily companions."

"But your gift will bring me peace with my prayers for the hours of darkness. I shall not forget you."

There were tears in the old man's eyes as Galahad knelt before him for the last time. Elaine smiled as he rose, but with the corner of his eye he saw Dame Brisen draw back into the angle of a buttress as if to escape his glance. "Poor woman," he thought, "perhaps she doesn't hate all the world, but fears it will reject her. Never offered, never refused." He went to her now and caught both her hands, drawing her from the corner.

"Dear madam," he began, "I have not always enjoyed your instruction, but I have always profited by it. Above all I thank you for your unfailing loyalty to my mother. God keep you." The old woman darted a quick glance at him with a little smile that told him she had not missed the allusion – a dark night, she leading Lancelot to a tower chamber. She put the back of the boy's hand to her wrinkled cheek a moment, but she said nothing.

Galahad turned now to his mount. It was a great white stallion, still with dappled buttocks. The youth had been practicing mounting in full armor – no easy assignment – and he managed it now with as much grace as he could. He saluted his mother and the priest and directed his steed out of the gate toward the north-east. The horse was eager for adventure and the two disappeared into the forest at a lively trot.

He was not at once to appear in Camelot. Instead he was to report to an abbey not far away. What he did not know was that an ab-bess headed the establishment, and although there were lay brothers for managing the lands and a couple of priests for celebrating mass and hearing confessions, it was a convent. He was less than pleased when he arrived. The novices were not permitted to talk to him and the older nuns had little to say to a handsome young warrior. Of course young and old tittered at his arrival, and they called him the best knight in the world. He interpreted this as a reference to his father and a hope that the convent might find distinction through him – a distinction it had never expected.

In the last two years Galahad received more intensive training in arms. His grandfa-ther, King Pelles, handicapped as he was by an old wound, could not himself help in his edu-cation, but he had regularly sent over a couple of younger men from Castle Corbin, only a mile or so from Joyeux Gard. Particularly in that first summer when he was sixteen, Galahad per-formed admirably. He had not yet his full growth, but he was quick and sure and he regu-larly tumbled his opponents. But at seventeen – that perfect summer when he met Keren – the tables were suddenly turned and Galahad found a seat in the grass with great consistency. These lads were older, one already a knight, the other soon to follow at his twentieth birthday. They would come to Joyeux Gard two or three times a week, and when he had left Keren, he would find them waiting for him. In the late afternoon or early evening they would have a go at each other, their lances blunted by great knobs of leather so that they would not penetrate.

By August, however, Galahad found his balance better, his seat more secure. Since the parting with Keren on Lugnasad, he wandered less and was home earlier for practice. But his companions arrived later and later. All of them laughed when anyone was unseated, but as August passed Galahad's laughter grew louder and longer and theirs became more and more perfunctory. By the autumn they had had enough of it and their visits dropped to once a week.

Even these young men were not allowed to linger. Galahad was promptly called away at evensong, so that he continued friendless and alone. He had looked forward to the final months of preparation for knighthood, hoping at last to find comrades. He was undisguisedly disappointed at his life in the abbey. But accustomed as he was to loneliness, he threw himself into the religious instruction with quiet determination. So excellent had been Father Peter's early training that by the following Easter he was told to prepare for knighthood at Pentecost.

It had been a long winter, but he had done

what he could to relieve the monotony. When he crossed the abbey yard to the chapel, or returned, or went to the refectory he would see the little girls who had come to be educated at the convent peering out at him from angles of doorways or over the tops of walls or even under hedges. They all giggled together, and then one more daring than the rest might cry out "Best knight in the world!" This always brought gales of laughter from the rest, and sooner or later one of the older nuns would shoo them all out of his path.

Finally he developed a game. When they shouted at him, he would stop short and bow low with a flourish of his hat or his hand in a salute worthy of an emperor. This brought still further appreciation from the giggling children. But the abbess once witnessed this and begged him not to. "We must bring them up as modest young girls whether they go into the Order or not. Please help us to maintain discipline." He obeyed her request, but he sometimes grinned or winked at the little faces. They never after did more than giggle, and he saw none of the bolder ones for the rest of his visit.

When Galahad knew exactly when he was to be knighted, he made his only request: that Lancelot bestow knighthood on him. Even though most of them knew of their relationship, they protested that it was a far greater honor for King Arthur to admit him to knighthood. That stubborn streak that Lancelot had noticed in the lad of six was not lacking in the young man of eighteen. They gave in to his request.

The night before, much as at his confir-
mation, Galahad watched all night in the chapel,
guarding his armor. He had, however, neither
sword nor shield nor lance, but only an empty
sheath. This again was in keeping with his own
choice, and also the instruction of the hermit
Nacien, a priest who visited the Abbey especially
to supervise these rites.

Galahad imposed less strict penance on
himself. He knelt some of the time and stood
some of the time. He even paced the chapel. For
he felt that this was more a military rite than a
religious rite, and since that summer at seventeen, he had had little enough to confess, even
of worldly thoughts. When the windows glim-
mered in the first gray of morning, he said his
final prayers.

As day was breaking a group of the ma-
ture nuns (whom, alas, he had found far from
interesting company) came for him. First they
led him to a bathhouse where he bathed. He
was then dressed in a tunic of red silk and
brought to the chapel. It was the Feast of Pentecost and for the first time in twelve years he
saw his father. The gaunt, unhappy, lonely
knight was now in excellent health. Only his
eyes had a wistfulness and his smile was a quiet
smile without mirth, without happiness.
Galahad expected to see him, but nevertheless,
he had wondered for a moment who this was
who entered with that confident stride.

First there was the ceremony: Galahad

bowed his golden head as he knelt before his father. The red silk tunic flushed his cheeks. Lancelot tapped him lightly on the shoulder with the flat of his sword and said, "Arise, Sir knight." As the boy rose the two looked at each other. They were of equal height and met each other's gaze directly. There was a slight pause, then Lancelot opened his arms and Galahad rushed into them. He had never approved of his father, and he had always been embarrassed by him. But he owed him so much – life, skill, and training in arms, even the reputation he had not yet earned. On his part Lancelot felt how much he owed the boy's mother, and what a splendid lad he had grown to be. He kissed his son on both cheeks and Galahad knelt once more before him. "Thank you, father," he said, "for this accolade and for all I have learned from you." Lancelot raised him with both hands. "God bless you, my son, and may you and your mother forgive me for what I could not do."

When Lancelot returned to Camelot, he found that the Siege Perilous had strange writing in gold, which by his calculation meant it was to find its proper knight that day. Arthur and the court had not yet come from the chapel, so Lancelot asked the servants to veil the siege until time to reveal it.

Shortly after Arthur entered the dininghall. He was at once reminded that it was not his custom to begin a great feast until he had seen a wonder. Just then a youth entered in some excitement, made his way to Arthur and told of a miraculous stone holding a sword and floating on the river. The court at once followed the lad to the spot. The stone was not actually floating in the river as the boy had reported, but it looked as if it might be floating, and there was certainly a sword thrust into it. On the pommel they read: "Never shall man take me hence but only he by whose side I ought to hang, and he shall be the best knight in the world."

Arthur laughed and said, "This should be soon solved. Come, Lancelot, I am sure you qualify."

Lancelot shook his head. "No, my lord," he replied, "this is not my sword and I am not so bold as to set hand to it. It has no wish to be mine. Whoever, knowing himself unworthy, attempts to draw it will be sorely wounded by it and will be lucky to survive."

Arthur then urged Gawaine to try, but Gawaine, too, refused. Arthur was annoyed. Would all his knights play this game of humility? Would the assemblage of the finest knights of the world become a laughingstock when none dared prove his worth? He turned petulant and commanded Gawaine to try. Gawaine felt that at last he might prove his superiority to Lancelot, and after saluting his king he grasped the sword in both hands, giving it a mighty tug. But the blade remained stuck fast. Next Arthur turned to Sir Percival, who he knew led a blameless life. Percival paused only a moment, then murmured, "I shall gladly follow Sir Gawaine into whatever danger." But though he grasped it strongly close to the blade and pulled his best, he had no more luck than Gawaine.

At this point Sir Kay mentioned to the king that this surely had been a marvel, and that the feast might begin. So chattering together about that curious adventure, they returned to the great hall with its Round Table. They seated themselves in their proper places and the young knights, who had not yet been tested, served them.

There were stacks of thick slices of bread that they used as plates, platters laden with roasted fowl, others with venison and boar, and besides there were tureens of soups and stews with bowls of pewter for serving them. The king and those about him had gold and silver before them. Beside these were goblets and flagons for the drink brought in in kegs and barrels and a great bustle of young knights and servants keeping bowls and platters and tankards brimming.

But while food was still being brought in, there came a clap of thunder, and windows and doors rattled and banged shut. The sky had not appreciably darkened, and they looked in wonder at each other. At the back of the hall there appeared an old hermit with a strange tonsure that swept his head from ear to ear. He led by the hand a young knight clad in a red silk tunic, without sword or shield, but with an empty scabbard by his side.

The hermit approached Arthur. "My Lord King," he said, this is the knight who shall bring most honor to the Round Table." Then he had the young man take off his armor revealing the red cloth that covered him from head to toe, and after placing an ermine cloak about his shoulders, he led him to the one vacant seat, the Siege Perilous. When the hermit withdrew the cloth Lancelot had placed over it, the seat now had on it the name of Galahad.

This dramatic entry had not been Galahad's idea at all, and he thought it an arrogant and unnecessary extravagance, but Donnán, once he had reappeared after the ceremony of the morning, had told him of what he had written already on the seat for Lancelot to discover. He had chuckled and rubbed his hands when he told of Lancelot's having covered it so that no one else had seen it.

"There's another bit of a matter, my lad," he said, rubbing his hands again. "A stone in its sitting there and the sword in its standing in it. Of course no stone it is, but the look of stone is on it. They'll be asking ye to draw the sword out, and others will be after trying it, perhaps that rascally father of yours. Whatever, remember this: put but the one hand to it, and that toward the knob at the back. It's likely to me they'll grasp it forward. If you pull and it is hard fast in it, move your hand back a bit and the sword should lift out easily."

"But father, why all this? I'll be no better and no worse for this, but they'll expect great things – even my 'rascally' father."

"No fear. It is the best knight in the world you are now for sure. Is no man escapes his destiny – not your father, not your mother, not you. They all are to mark that and to let you get on at once with all you are after being put in this world for. No long life will be yours." (Galahad remembered that Cú Chulainn had deliberately chosen to take arms on a day when he would be splendid and famous though short-lived.) "Play your part, lad, and trust me," Donnán added. "I have a bit of writing to do."

After prayers at six o'clock the hermit had reappeared to take Galahad to the Round Table. Donnán chuckled as he heard the sudden storm blowing the windows. "It isn't the doors they'll be watching now. Slip in while there are other thoughts in them.

Galahad was frankly blushing as he saw his name on the Siege Perilous. He hoped that the red clothes he wore would seem to be reflected in his face, and that none would know what an impious imposter he felt himself to be. Fortunately, there was such chattering among the knights that Galahad did not need to utter a word. Lancelot, beside him, was staring at him in bewilderment and pride, and gave his arm an encouraging pat. After dinner at Arthur's insistence, they all filed out to view again the miraculous sword and stone. Galahad saw how cleverly it had been made. The wine and the good food as well as his father's presence had put heart into him, and with inner amusement he assumed the role of miracle-worker, according to instructions.

First King Arthur explained how others

had failed and that Lancelot would not try. He thought to himself, "My father is a man of integrity. He is a good man, but Mal Fete-star-crossed. He said in what he assumed to be a properly solemn, formal delivery, "Sir, that is no marvel, for this adventure is not theirs, but mine, and for the surety of this sword I brought none with me; for here by my side hangs the scabbard."

With that he grasped the sword with one hand, high on the hilt, and the sword slipped easily forth. He recited for them then the origin of the sword as the hermit had told it to him. He executed this duty with more grace than his inner discomfort expected. But there followed on this recital a scene that added to his personal distaste for the performance.

A young girl came riding up along the riverbank, and before them all laughed at his father – well, strictly speaking, she wept, but the mockery was as pointed. She cried out that he had been the best knight in the world until today, but now as the adventure of the sword showed, there was one better.

Lancelot's voice was low and steady as he replied: "As for that, I know well that I was never the best." The humility of tone surprized the boy who had always thought his father must be proud and satisfied, since his praise was on everyone's lips. The girl was speaking again: "Yes, but that were you, and are yet of any sinful man of the world." She stressed"sinful" and Lancelot looked at her steadily with his deep gray eyes, but he said no more.

The maiden then turned to King Arthur and foretold the coming of the Holy Grail to signalize that the company of the Round Table were the most worthy knights of the world. Galahad wondered if she had not been doing more planning with the Irish hermit, though she mentioned only Nacien.

King Arthur had planned a great tournament for Camelot. Galahad was shy about attending. He had been knighted, to be sure, but he had neither shield nor lance, and he was completely untried. Arthur, however, foresaw the problem and arranged a tourney, and offered to lend Galahad the equipment that he needed. At least the boy had a sword.

Galahad knew less than most of his contemporaries, knights or churls, of Camelot, for he had always felt embarrassment at asking much about it, and the servants whom he overheard were more interested in persons of rank and their exploits than in much of the actual life of the capital city. Had Galahad known that prophecies were to be fulfilled this day, he would not have assumed that his destiny was to fulfill them and that for this he had been knighted today. He knew that he was lucky; he did not know that a large measure of that luck lay in his contentment with whatever happened, his refusal to be concerned or troubled about matters where he had no choice but to accept. He would never have spent (he would have said "wasted") the last six months in a nunnery if he could have escaped it. But he lived unruffled through it all and now it was over.

He found himself whistling as he was fastened into cuirass, jambeaux, gauntlets and the rest of his armor. Dame Brisen used to tell him that whistling was unseemly, but though he had begun by imitating the stable boys, he could see no wrong in it. She had muttered something about God and sacred music, and he had proceeded to whistle hymns for her. He did not believe God was dismayed by trivial expressions of light-heartedness.

Yet for six months now he had not felt like whistling. But at last he was a knight; he was free to come and go; he was about to enter the first tournament of his life – the first he had ever seen. He was too ashamed of his ignorance to ask questions, but he watched and listened and was careful not to be the first to ride out. He had qualms, too. He was totally untried. Indeed Arthur's first aim had been to give the new knights an opportunity to prove themselves. All his life Galahad, who seemed so sure of himself, merely concealed his questions behind a façade of serenity. At any moment, he thought, his luck might run out.

Now as he saw his father on a great black stallion come galloping onto the field, banners flying, plumes fluttering, armor resounding, he felt a thrill of anticipation. Lancelot's steed trotted around the field with assurance, and paused before the royal couple. He raised his lance in salute and then trotted on. Gawaine followed with his brothers Agravaine, Gaheris, and Gareth close behind. Bedivere and Kay, Percival de Galis and Bors, Ector, one by one they rode forth, saluted and then took their places at one end or the other of the field. In these festive tourneys it would all be a general mélée, and individual prowess was rated above teamwork. But in the first rush, one side would assault the other.

Galahad leaned slightly forward, set his lance in the feuter, dug his knees into the heavy saddle, and touched the white flanks of his mount with his spurs. This was the stallion's first tournament too, but he leapt forward as if he had been waiting eagerly for the signal, and he kept pace with the last horse that had entered the field before him. Inside the helmet, even with the visor raised, Galahad could not hear what the heralds were shouting, and the noises of the field and the crowd seemed remote. The trumpets sounded, the heralds shouted as each knight paused before the royal box. Galahad followed in the line circling the field, and when he could glimpse the scarlet banner with the golden dragon he drew his horse to a halt and raised the point of his lance in salute. No ladies dined in the great hall so that this was his first glimpse of Guenever, sitting beside Arthur. At that distance he got no more than an impression of the long golden braids and the regal bearing. Then off he trotted to the side of the field where Lancelot and Percival waited, Perhaps a dozen other riders followed him, but now he had closed his visor and through the narrow slit he could see almost nothing.

The blare of trumpets sounded the charge and Lancelot and Percival led the assault with Gawaine and his brothers (except for Gareth, who would not ride against Lancelot even in play) leading from the opposite side. Galahad never enjoyed anything so much as that first tournament. It was not just that his seat was sure, his horse powerful and obedient, and he was toppling everyone who opposed him, but the noise and sweat and physical exercise after days and nights of prayer, hymns, and sermons with a chorus of giggling girls gave a wild joy and sense of freedom that he was never to feel again. Brotherhood, companionship, after eighteen years of solitude. Not for long, but this once, it was his heart's desire.

When Galahad saw what havoc he could wreak with that borrowed lance, he began assaulting only the older knights. But the younger, knowing from his blank shield that he must be unpracticed, would attack him and seemed not to notice that he was unseating everyone he met. Three knights he carefully avoided – his father, Ector, and Percival, whom he had seen at Joyeux Gard so very long ago.

Part of the fun had been the bloodlessness of the combat. As soon as unhorsed, a knight gave up and left the field. There was no followup with swords as there would have been in battle. Even so it was a rough sport. Occasionally there were broken bones, and a few knights, badly stunned, had to be carried off the field rather than leading their mounts away.

Galahad was panting, the damp hair clung to his brow, when Guenever summoned him at the end of the day. At last he could see this queen who had cast such a long shadow over Joyeux Gard. He attended her, his helmet on his hip, but without the sweat or the exhilaration of battle removed. She stood beside King Arthur, and both watched him kneel, but only she spoke.

"I well think you Lancelot's son," she said, "for twenty years ago he would have been your exact image. It is no wonder you have shown such prowess today."

She reached out her hand with the deep red ruby, and raised him to his feet. He could look full at her. Yes, she was more beautiful, more colorful than his mother. Elaine was so pale a blonde that except when she darkened her brows and lashes with charcoal, as she sometimes did on feast days, she was pale, almost faded with her doll-like daintiness and pale yellow hair. Guenever's hair was a rich gold in braids to her knees, hanging before her shoulders against that dark red gown. Her brows and lashes were dark brown and her eyes a deep liquid blue like midnight skies. She had grace and dignity. Everyone talked about Elaine's beauty, but beside Guenever, it was the beauty of a white daisy or a waterlily beside that of a yellow rose or a yellow flag of the marshlands.

Galahad bowed and backed from her presence. At the door stood his father, who smiled at him. He read in that smile pride and admiration and affection. He also noted that though his features resembled his father and his height was the same, that he had inherited from his mother also and was a paler version with sunnier hair, not brown; blue-gray eyes, not gray, and he had not yet tried to grow a beard. Indeed he thought it would be gold or red, and he doubted that it would suit him.

Galahad spent that evening talking with his fellow knights. Only Gareth, Percival, and Bors seemed at ease with him. He could see that to the others he was an interloper. As he crawled at last into bed he realized that solitude was a part of him. It was his way and his happiness.

Chapter VII

Knights Errant

Here I ame and fourthe I mouste,
& in Iesus Criste is all my trust.
No wicked thing do me no dare,
Nother here nor Elles whare.
The Father with me; the Sonne with me;
The Holly Goste, & the Trienete,
Be by-twyxte my gostely Enime & me.
In the name of the Father, & the Sonne
And the Holly Goste, Amen.

Middle English lyric

alahad was now a knight, as free as he ever would be. But he was beginning to realize that he was still a prisoner – a prisoner of his own character, of his own destiny, if those were two and not one. He could never find true comradeship. There in his first tournament he had felt it, but even then he had sat in the Siege Perilous unscathed and drawn that ominous weapon from the stone. Now after toppling all opponents, he could see men withdrawing from him. The older knights did not, but they were his father's generation and expected before too many years had passed to see greater prowess in the young while their experience and wisdom yet held for them a respected place at court. But to the young men, what could he say? If he said, "I didn't really expect to do so well," or "I'm sorry that stroke was so unlucky for you," they would scorn his insincerity. Only if he were indeed the "Best Knight in the World" could they justify to their pride his having overcome them. The readiness with which they accepted him as the best of them all, he recognized as their way of saving face.

Lancelot, on the other hand, had won his place – and of course Galahad's as well – by earning it in fair combat with his skill, his quickness, his strength of arm. He had won his place slowly, step by step, and had been able to make staunch friends as he went, for he was kind and generous, never pursuing an advantage to crush an opponent he knew to be inferior, gauged by his horsemanship, the force of his blows, and the courage he displayed. Galahad felt keenly that his luck made him less a man than his father. What had he known of the suffering of guilt? It seemed to him unfair that he had the acclaim. Having to face the transfer of glory to his son was not a small punishment for the one time "Best Knight of the World."

At the Pentecostal Feast that closed the day of the tournament yet another miracle was in store. As the knights sat in their appointed seats at the Round Table, there came a clap of thunder, a sudden breeze swirled along the tapestried wall – a breeze laden with the fragrance of herbs and flowers and the damp sweet air of spring. The company fell silent as they looked at one another in wonder, as a vessel shrouded in white samite moved through the hall. When it had passed they could hear outside a choir of clear high voices singing Hosanna.

For Galahad the event almost shattered the solemnity of the feast. He had caught sight of little feet below the white samite, and recognized the last pair and their limp. A year or so before he came to the convent, parents had brought their daughter, a child of five or six. They were ashamed of her club foot, and though the nuns assured them that this was God's mark of blessedness, the parents never returned. The girl was quick at learning her prayers, skilled in needlework beyond her years, and her sweet, true voice had been much in demand. Galahad was never permitted to talk with any but the older nuns, but her impish smile and sunny disposition had gladdened the play of the children and he too had felt happier for her presence. In spite of seeing Donnán's hand in this miracle, too, Galahad shared with the others the glow of friendship, happiness, and peace that settled on all the knights as the Grail passed through the hall.

The wine had been unusually heady. In the exhilaration that seized them all, Gawaine had been the first to jump to his feet and vow to seek throughout the world at least for a year, hoping to see the Grail uncovered. The rest had followed his lead. Then Arthur, who had perhaps drunk even more freely than they, what with having to answer so many more toasts, Arthur had wept and foretold that never again would his one hundred and fifty splendid champions be seated here. He had seen truly.

When word of these vows reached Guenever, she sent for the hermit Nacien and asked that the married and betrothed might accompany their men. This was, of course, denied them, for the Grail Quest was to succeed only for the purest and was to bring death or maiming to the most unworthy. When Galahad saw the weeping and unhappiness that followed on this announcement, he was again happy to be leaving no one behind, and sought out the little cluster of single knights – mostly young like himself – to plan for the departure next day.

Percival, Bors, Galahad and a handful of

others were seated in the chimney corner when a messenger came up requesting that Galahad attend the queen. As he followed the servant he wondered if she shared Arthur's forebodings of the outcome. She received him in that same room where Lancelot had spoken with her that time he was driven mad with despair; but the sunnyhaired baby who had lain at her feet that day of course remembered nothing of it.

Now Guenever asked him again of his origin. It was as if she hoped she might find a reason to doubt his parenthood, and yet she seemed to insist on it, to repeat it. When he said nothing, she praised Lancelot to him – a father to be proud of, his very image. But Galahad felt that to name his father would be to try to assume his protection and his glory. At last he said rather stiffly, "Madam, if you know that for certain, why do you ask me? When the time comes, who he is will not be hidden."

He looked her straight in the eyes, and her deep blue ones fell before his steady blue-gray ones. She said softly, "Your mother must be very proud of you. You are such a son as any woman would be happy to claim."

Galahad remembered kitchen prattle – "the barren queen" they had called her. "My mother is not a proud woman," he said. "I think she was glad to see me go that she might enter the church as she had hoped to do for so long. Children can warp a woman's destiny."

"May she be happy," said the queen. "I am sure that she thanks God that you were given to her."

She held out her hand. He knelt and kissed the solitary sapphire ring that she wore and then backed out of the room.

Galahad could scarcely be expected to react warmly to this adulteress who had kept his father ensnared all the years of his life. But he tried to get himself and his mother out of his head. What had his father seen in this woman, wife of the king to whom he had sworn loyalty? He saw a woman, beautiful beyond compare. His mother's pale primrose beauty faded beside the queen's splendid brows, tall form, and her grace and dignity. Every movement revealed her character and independence. She would ask no mercy of destiny. Perhaps she even loved Arthur in the way a person may love more than one – two sons, two sisters, two horses, two hounds.

His chief impression at that last audience with the queen was the sense of her intelligence, independence and strength. She had not tried to charm him or mother him, but had looked straight from her midnight eyes directly through him to his heart. In such a woman was indeed a charm beyond all smiles and banter. To be singled out by such a woman! Galahad understood as never before what power had overthrown his father's loyalty to his king, and had forever kept him true to one woman.

But though he could understand her love for two men, he could not understand how she could betray the king, or how his father, too, could live this double life. Galahad liked to believe in people. He had a generous and a humble heart. Arthur dazzled him. That would be a father to be proud of. That thought was in his mind as he left the audience with the queen. As he turned from the room he came face to face with Mordred, hidden in the shadow of the door. He had not heard the court scandal, and merely noted the suggestion of a sneer on his lips and his frowning brows. "Another lonely and unhappy man," he thought.

Galahad did not return to his new friends. He had too much to think over. Like the other young knights he rolled in a blanket on a bench in the great hall and lay thinking of the strange events of that day until long past midnight. When he said his prayers, he did not forget an appeal for Donnán. Then smiling, he dropped off to sleep.

The following morning with due weeping and praying and a reassertion of their vows, the flower of knighthood rode out of Camelot in a body. Lancelot had sought out Guenever in her chamber, and though she protested his going ("leaving his king" was the way she phrased it), she ended by giving him her blessing.

Galahad rode with the rest to a castle where in the hall and the village the knights all spent the night. In the morning, however, they agreed each to go his own way. This ride and that night of fellowship had convinced Galahad that companionship was not to be his, and he was rather sure that he preferred solitary adventures. All the earlier part of his life he had been alone, or at least almost completely without boys of his own age. In this short time he noticed many little things that he had escaped by his isolation. There were sycophants who wanted to be included in this or that retinue for its prestige. There were the petty jealousies between factions. Even among the leaders was pride and an insistence on forms of respect, due only to the very highest.

Galahad was happy to see his father aloof from this while lesser men squabbled for the chance to be one of his men. Galahad under no circumstances would have joined that group. How could a man find his own value under that protecting arm, under that superb gentleness, kindness, and humility? Lancelot always treated the lowliest with respect (Gareth knew especially) and they rated themselves, then, as very fine fellows indeed. Though he would not join him, Galahad respected him the more.

Now that the decision had been for chiefly individual quests, Galahad found himself more at ease, not fearing that others would find him too eager, too indifferent, too friendly, or too withdrawn. He rode off into lands drained by the Afon where the May warmth had brought out a carpet of purple and yellow flowers and the hedges bloomed with thorn trees and the golden gorse and broom gave grace to the wastelands. Larks bounded skyward pouring out floods of cascading song and the roadside quivered with the flutter of wings of chaffinches, titmice, and complaining twitters of wrens.

Galahad still had no shield and had refused any that had been offered. The weight of
the sword beside him was enough of an encum-
brance. The weapons must suit the man, and
without an heirloom weapon from his father,
Galahad awaited his shield patiently. Yet he was
happy after four days of riding northward when
he came to an abbey lying all freshly white-
washed in a little valley. The monks offered him
shelter and showed him into a room where two
knights sat eating a simple supper before a fire,
recently kindled, that took from the room the
chill that the evening brought. Galahad remembered the men vaguely and was not surprised
to hear they were of Arthur's court – Sir Uwaine
and King Bagdemagus.

Galahad found himself warmly welcomed
and wondered if these were ones he had pursued in the tourney. A lay brother set before
him a bowl of soup, a thick slice of bread and a
mug of thick brown ale. As they ate, the king
and Uwaine told of a shield in that castle that
was said to bring trouble or death to any who
bore it until its rightful owner should find it.

"It is worth a try," said the lad. "I have
been looking for a shield. If it is not mine, I'll
soon know it."

"This can be a dangerous adventure; it's
not for a lad." Bagdemagus, experienced and
outranking the others, could claim the right if
he wished.

"My lord," put in Uwaine, "we have ridden together these past three days and have

seen nothing more exciting than a herd of roedeer and warrens of rabbits. If the boy is so foolish, let him get his head cracked."

"If it were chasing deer and rabbits, I'd gladly surrender the privilege," said the king. "But this will be a break with boredom and I shall assay it first. If I have no luck in this, then either of you may follow your own fortune."

Galahad was uneasy. He felt sure the king would suffer, perhaps die for his foolhardiness, but a lad of eighteen, newly dubbed a knight, does not tell a king of fifty to be cautious.

After mass the next morning the king asked to be shown the shield. A monk brought it out from behind the altar. When he saw it, Galahad knew at once it was his. He longed for it on his shoulder. Bagdemagus picked it up, looked critically at the design – a red cross on a gleaming white field – and said as he weighed it, "It is light for a warrior's; perhaps it is for a child after all." Nevertheless, he slung on his shoulder and it flashed white in the dusky chapel, the cross seeming to burn.

The monk looked troubled and cautioned him that this shield might be borne only by the best knight in the world. Bagdemagus chuckled. "I know well that I am not the best knight in the world, and yet I shall make a trial of it. Galahad, wait here and my squire will return to tell you whether or not to seek the adventure." King and squire mounted and rode jauntily out of the chapel gate.

Hardly half an hour later they returned, the king in great pain. His right shoulder, not protected by the shield, had been struck through by a spear. The monks helped them bear him to an inner chamber, and one of them began cleaning the wound. But the squire went to Sir Galahad and offered him the shield, saying, "My lord Galahad, he who wounded my master sends you greeting and asks that you bear this shield." Galahad took it gladly. He wondered if the others too saw a pulsing flaming cross on a shimmering ground of snow. "If I am indeed the best knight of the world, this miracle will prove it without help from my Irish friend. And if I am not, I shall have some sense knocked into my head."

He commended King Bagdemagus to Sir Uwaine and started to mount, but Sir Uwaine wished to accompany him. "Perhaps my luck will be no better than the king's," he said. "Stay and watch by him but let his squire ride with me. He can bring you word if I fail."

The squire was beaming with delight, and scrambled into the saddle almost before Galahad could mount himself. He then spurred his sorrel past Galahad to guide him on the road to a chapel not two miles away where he said the king had been wounded. A knight in white armor greeted them and asked them into the chapel. He seemed not to have many visitors and to be longing to talk with someone. The story of the history of the shield Galahad found interesting. The accoutrements of a knight were representative of his lineage in the blazon and of his quality as a warrior in their excellence. Galahad, who had not been armed by his father, whose family was no family, looked on these instruments as his title. He did smile on hearing that the sacred blood with which the cross had been painted was blood that Joseph of Arimathea had shed in a nosebleed before he died. When he was alone he examined the cross, and was not surprised to find a high quality of paint and no evidence of anything else. His experiences with Donnán made him somewhat sceptical of wonders. Nevertheless, he felt the shield suited him and he knew now that, like his sword, it was an heirloom.

Meanwhile, once the history of the shield was told, the squire, his eyes big with awe, stabled his sorrel gelding and begged Galahad to grant him knighthood. It was only the second week since he himself had been knighted, but the boy was so earnest and full of wonder that Galahad smiled and said, "Tomorrow, then."

About the rest of the events of that day, Galahad was never sure. There was something about a tomb that gave out a frightening noise and a terrible stench. He was asked to open it and a gruff, harsh voice cried out against the band of angels that clustered about Galahad's head. Then someone explained about the body in the tomb being the duress of the world and what hard times had fallen on the country. Since next he knew the sun was pouring in his eastern window, he suspected he had dreamed the whole thing. It was an insistent and very real dream that haunted him the next day. By the headache he had, he thought he had sipped much more mead than he realized as the knight spun out the history of the shield.

Part of his recollection was accurate, however, for here was the squire, his face beaming, eager to help him dress, and reminding him that today he was to be knighted.

"Have you kept vigil?" Galahad asked, his head pounding.

"Oh, yes, my lord, all night in the chapel."

"You realize that knights are not common soldiers. What is your name and lineage that I may perform the ceremony properly?"

"They call me Melias de Lile, and my father is king of Denmark."

In spite of his headache Galahad burst out laughing. "My boy, when I have knighted you, you will outrank me, for I am no king's son and a bastard at that."

The boy replied solemnly, "But sir, you are the best knight in the world and there is no higher rank than that."

So the squire became Sir Melias de Lile, and Galahad asked him to do in all things according to the rules of chivalry, especially because as king's son he should be a pattern to the world. But the boy had yet another request, that he might go with Galahad in search of the Holy Grail. As his first request after achieving knighthood, this could not be denied. King

Bagdemagus, through Uwaine, presented the boy with armor, spear and a great bay stallion. Melias climbed eagerly to the saddle and the two rode forth.

For a week they wandered among rolling hills, finding shelter at night in villages or castles or in the lee of a hill that rose against the wind. On the eighth day, a Monday, they came to a fork in the road. No gate or trail is more fascinating than one labeled "No admittance." At the crossroads was a sign cautioning adventurers that few who took the lefthand way would return again "but if he be a good man and a worthy knight."

"What better way to prove myself," said Melias confidently.

"Wouldn't it be better if I took that way?" cautioned Galahad. "I have not seen much action, but I have been in a tournament; I have won sword and shield. You go to the right and I'll go to the left and take a chance on the adventures that I meet."

"No," replied Melias, "please let me make the attempt. How shall I know what I am worth if I leave every adventure to you?"

Galahad did not know what lay ahead. He was trading on his past good luck to help the boy. Alone he would surely have taken the lefthand path for all the reasons Melias gave him. He could not deny him what he wished for himself. "Go your way, in God's name," he said.

The righthand trail led into a quiet forest. Gray boles of beech trees stood like great columns beside the way and the sun, filtering through the green crown of the woods cast golden images of the sun like scattered coins on the forest floor. The murmur of doves, a brook somewhere chuckling, and a nightingale pouring out his heart seemed like an unearthly choir. But after some hours Galahad was sated with the calm and restfulness. He touched the near flank of his white stallion and trotted back the way he had come. This time he took the lefthand way, urging his steed at a lively trot to try to catch Sir Melias.

Night fell before he found his fellow, and it was well into the next day before he saw him, badly wounded, a spear still lodged in his side. He leapt from his horse and knelt beside him. Melias, his brow damp with the sweat of suffering, recognized him. "Sir," he moaned, "for God's love let me not die in this forest, but bear me to the abbey nearby, that I may be confessed and have my rites."

Galahad remembered where he had passed the little vinecovered chapel perhaps a mile away, and he promised to do as he wished. Just then, however, someone called out and Melias gave warning that this was the knight who had wounded him. The encounter was not easy, even for the best knight in the world. For the first time he was fighting in earnest. They feutered their lances and rushed together. His lance caught the other on the shoulder, just as he had hoped, and the other tumbled to the ground. But the lance had penetrated his shoulder and as he fell it bent, then snapped. Galahad tossed the butt from him just as another knight rushed from a thicket before he could draw his sword. The new adversary charged straight at the crimson cross in the center of Galahad's shield. Galahad clutched the pommel of his saddle to withstand the force of the blow and now his opponent's spear snapped. Galahad could now draw his sword as the horse plunged past him. For the first time since he drew it from the stone the sword was unsheathed for battle. By now the other had wheeled his mount and was bearing down on him, sword at the ready. As they met Galahad swung his blade with his full force, evading the other's parry. His weapon caught the knight just above the elbow and sheared the arm off. He had no time for thought as the arm lay there on the ground and blood gushed in arterial pulses over horse and rider. His horse meanwhile wheeled and gave chase. But Galahad sickened as he saw what he had done, and he turned back to Sir Melias.

Melias was still conscious and Galahad took him in his arms, feeling himself the misery of that unfortunate man, the truncheon of the spear still in his side. Galahad lifted him to the horse's back, holding him as they rode slowly back to the abbey where Melias had asked to be confessed. He had clenched his teeth as they rode, and Galahad prayed that he might swoon, but that prayer was denied.

As gently as he could, Galahad bore him in his arms to a chamber of the abbey that the priest indicated and asked for housel. As soon as the wounded man tasted the wine and wafer, he revived a bit, saying to Galahad: "Sir, let death come when it pleases him." Immediately afterward he drew the truncheon from his own body and lost consciousness. An old monk then approached and examined the wound. "God willing," he said, "I can heal him, perhaps in two months or less. I have been a knight myself and the wound is clean."

Galahad stayed at the abbey three days until Sir Melias could assure him he was better. Then he announced his intention to continue his quest for the Grail. One of the monks stopped him at the gate. He was tall and straight, and Galahad at once liked the frankness of his gaze. "Sir," he said, "this man was wounded because of sin. He has not made a full confession. The righthand way is the way of the Lord, and therefore have you found it unadventurous. But the other is the way of sinners and unbelievers. It was pride that made Melias wish to seek the Holy Grail; then later where you found him, he had taken a golden crown that lay among foods he might have stolen, but did not wish. These two sins, pride and covetousness, are the two knights with whom you fought. Good fortune is yours, Galahad, for you are without deadly sin."

Galahad said quietly,"In my heart I have committed many sins, but I have repented them all, even the thinking of them. Assure Melias that when he is healed I hope to meet him again."

"Be confident that he will seek you as soon as he can ride. He has no fever now."

Thereupon Galahad commended them all to God and rode off alone.

Some say that Galahad heard of the Castle of Maidens while he was at prayer, but in truth he had heard of it at every inn or abbey or lonely farm as he turned now west to the Severn and then northward along it. When he arrived at the castle which he instantly recognized from the descriptions he had heard, he wasted no time in driving out the seven knights who had held all passers-by in bondage and oppressed them all under their sway. The knights had charged him one after the other, but one after the other their lances had shattered on the crimson cross of his shield.

Galahad himself found it disappointing. To destroy sin is good, but simply to chase it elsewhere leaves little satisfaction. Brooding on this he turned his horse back toward the Afon and the abbey where he had left Sir Melias. In the month that had passed he should have recovered. Indeed, when Galahad stooped through the low door of the abbey, there sat Sir Melias chatting with Gawaine. Their greeting was warm and friendly and they listened while Galahad told of his adventures.

"You merely drove them out?" cried Gawaine incredulously. "I would run the rascals down and destroy them before they do more mischief."

"That would be real sport," agreed Melias.

"I do what I must," said Galahad, "but slaughter and pain give me no pleasure."

"That is man's work," replied Gawaine. "If you can't manage it, there are those who will."

Galahad began to see what those at Camelot knew well, that Gawaine was a bitter and a jealous man who throve on violence. He had once been acclaimed "best knight of the world" and, as his nephew, had stood at the king's right hand. Then Lancelot came riding, fresh from France. He asked no favors, insulted no one, but he accepted all challenges and without exception was victorious. Suddenly at tournaments and festivals the crowds were all chanting: "Lancelot! Lancelot!   Best Knight of all!" Until last Pentecost, Gawaine had looked on Lancelot as his arch-rival. Now this beardless boy was suddenly hailed as a nine-day's-wonder. Though delighted that Lancelot was displaced, Gawaine felt a worse sting that a mere stripling was "best knight of the world." He had followed on his track to see what the lad was worth. He felt now he knew.

A priest tried to explain to Gawaine that the seven knights were the seven deadly sins and the prisoners were those dying before the coming of Christ. Galahad was like Christ harrowing Hell. But Gawaine hardly listened and rode off next morning straight toward the Severn with Uwaine and his youngest brother Gareth. They found the seven knights in the corner of a tavern eating their supper. The three set on the seven and cut them to ribbons and Gawaine went to bed happy that he had shown the world who the best knight was.

Galahad noticed that Melias, though still weak when he had returned, was visibly improved by the next morning when Gawaine had galloped westward. "It is not my virtue," he thought, but Melias' belief in my virtue that gives him life." As he had accepted the Siege Perilous and the sword in the stone, the shield of the "best knight of the world," so he resigned himself to this role – not for his own sake, but for those who trusted him. To those who believed in him, he would give succor. The cost to himself was small compared to the good to them. But it took its toll in psychological exhaustion, and as they strengthened, he would weaken. Had he known this, he would not have held back. He had the courage of Lancelot and the devotion of Elaine, and he was more selfless than either. As few can ever manage to do, he set his own happiness, his own will, last. In this he was most blessed and most hurt: Heaven achieved would be his reward without riches or power in this world, nor the ways of joy men here long for. He remained a bastard – a blessed bastard – denied the inheritance of this world's good, overwhelmed by the showering gold of God.

Chapter VIII

Fathers and Sons

Go to Rome?
Great pains, small gain they give you:
the King you seek there none find
unless you bring him with you.

[From the Irish *Codex Boernerianus*]

Wailing birds; wet ground in sight;
leaves fall: lone the homeless plight.
No denial, I'm ill tonight.

[From the Welsh of Llywarch Hen]

Galahad rode northward toward the Scottish border now. As the hills grew higher and the valleys steeper, the forests   grew denser. But there were clearings here and there and a well marked way. He was approaching the great Caledonian Forest and oak and aspen were giving way to pine and birch. He had just thought to himself, "It is the first of August – Lugnasad," when he saw entering a clearing from the opposite direction, Lancelot and Percival de Galis. He was about to hail them when his father feutered his lance and galloped straight for him.

He had just time to lower his visor, couch his lance and meet the onset as best he could. Lancelot's spear caught just where it ought to catch, but instead of carrying his opponent off over the crupper as he expected, it snapped off while Galahad's spear held and sent him rolling, his horse slipping and falling at the same time. Galahad acquired his shield after he had last seen his father, but Lancelot might have recognized the white stallion and the crimson tunic of his son.

But now Percival had drawn his sword and was riding at Galahad from the other side. "Dear God," prayed the boy, "don't let me hurt him!" But again he must meet the attack as best he could. His lighter weight and younger destrier combined to give him an advantage, to maneuver his mount to parry the first blow and bring his blade crashing down on Percival's helmet. The force knocked Sir Percival too to the ground, senseless and bleeding.

A recluse had watched the whole swift combat from her hut at the edge of the clearing, and now she cried out: "God be with thee, best knight of the world!   Had yon knights known thee as I do, they would not have encountered thee." Galahad recognized one of the older nuns, one who had sometimes reproved the bolder girls who shouted at him. But he had seen a twinkle of amusement even then at his salute. Now he raised his sword in an abbreviated salute and rode off before Lancelot could catch his horse. Much as he would have liked to talk with them under other circumstances, he thought it best to go unrecognized.

Lancelot mounted and pursued his son, but already the boy had far outdistanced him and he soon turned back to see how badly wounded Percival might be. After the sheer amazement at something that had not happened to him since years before his knighthood, what he felt was pride. As he hit the ground he had realized who the knight must be. "My son, my boy – how splendid he is!" he exclaimed. He was chuckling as he rode off after him. And this was the beginning of the adventures that were to humble him so that he might at last have the clearest view of the Grail of any except those most perfect three, only one of whom was to bring back the story of it.

And Galahad? His mind was in confusion. Was he indeed the best knight in the world? It was the first moment that it had occurred to

him that perhaps it might be so. Had he been
able to see under the helm Lancelot's open-
mouthed astonishment at being unseated, he
would not only have laughed aloud, but he
would have felt that something near the miraculous had happened. But he saw none of that
and found instead that he was trying to explain
it away. His father had inferior equipment; his
lance had shattered and his horse had
stumbled. Galahad admitted even then a thrill
of satisfaction. He had sincerely wished to avoid
any such meeting if he could. It was not his
fault that they charged an unknown knight
without challenge or identification. Moreover,
all his life he had heard again and again that
his father was the best knight in the world.
Lancelot certainly was not the best father, and
the boy had been well aware of his mother's re-
sentment toward him. He had in his younger
days felt the bitterness, too, and although now
he had begun to see his father in a different
light, this victory was sweet. He knew his mother
would have clapped her hands.

When Lancelot returned to Percival, he
found him beginning to gain consciousness, but
the sword that Percival had tried in vain to draw
from the stone had bitten to the bone. Lancelot
found a hermit not far away who was skilled in
leechcraft, and he waited by his side until he
was sure he was improving. In the evenings,
shortening now toward summer's end, he talked
to the hermit about what had chanced. The
hermit at once confirmed that it was his son

who had unseated him, and added a word of caution "to in no place press not upon him to have ado with him."

Lancelot had no thought of vengeance, and said, "it is my hope that that good knight should pray for me to the high Father that I may not fall again into sin." The hermit assured him that he had the prayers of Galahad and all decent men.

But he added more sharply: "Neither father nor son bears the sins of the other, but each must pray to the heavenly Father. He will suffice to give us help as we need."

Lancelot saw then that though the boy had been conceived in deceit, though he had thought he was committing a yet greater sin, and though afterwards he had steadily refused to marry the boy's mother because he was so bound to – even so happy in – his adultery, that these were his sins, and no part in any way a blemish for the child. As the hermit had said: "Every each shall bear his own burthen." In this Lancelot saw yet more. Children are good or bad in their own way. Our pride in them is no more justified than our shame for what they do. Even his almost total separation from his son had not made the boy unlike him, nor had the boy learned from Elaine to seek by guile what he could not have in fairness. In his heart Lancelot thanked God that this was so – that his son had not suffered from his guilt.

Galahad, always a solitary lad, enjoyed the life of a knight. Because he was so used to being alone, he found casual encounters, a night spent in prayer with a hermit, or perhaps watching by one lying ill in his castle, were sufficient renewal of human contacts – a spiritual refreshener too. One time he chanced on Sir Percival in sharp combat with twenty knights. He had rushed in on his white stallion and had sent them flying. When his lance broke, he tossed the splintered shaft from him and drew his sword. Though the odds had seemed overwhelming, the knights thinned out rapidly under his attack until the remnant took flight and he galloped off in pursuit, leaving Percival shouting his thanks after him.

To those of the Round Table, Galahad was a mysterious figure. No sooner had he come among them than they had all scattered in individual quests for the Holy Grail. They sometimes glimpsed a red-clad warrior on a snow-white destrier bearing a white shield with a crimson cross. If they attacked him, he would tumble them from the saddle; perhaps like Percival, they would see him drive off their foes when they were hard pressed; but they rarely met him in taverns and in any group he listened more than he spoke.

What would he talk about? He had grown up hearing only servants' talk of the court, and that was as full of fancy as their tales of ghosts and dragons and fairyland. They had as little interest in his quiet country life as he in their brawling and boasting. He did not look back, but rather forward to the hope of the perfect fellowship of the Round Table – still so far from its goal. He was not naive enough to believe this world would ever reach perfection, but he was determined to live as honorably as he could. Knighthood had made him feel that he was no longer too young to bother about injustice, too young to suppress violence when he could, and he accepted what he conceived to be his role meekly, as he had always done.

The knights of the Round Table, it seemed to Galahad, were only half tamed, half civilized. Some of them understood part of Arthur's great dream, but more found the organization fine backing for their arrogance and selfishness. He understood more and more why his father was the best of them. He saw, too, that the devotion to God and his worship that had been so large a part of his own life, mattered to very few of these. To Sir Percival, Sir Bors, and his father the Christian way had meaning, but not to the violent Gawaine, the great lover Tristram and the lesser men. Peace and happiness he found only when he felt the presence of God and the way to that was a lonely road. He did not despise others for their different values, he merely accepted that they had little in common.

From the northern forests Galahad wandered south, criss-crossing the country as chance led him. In a quiet wooded valley of western Mercia or eastern Powys, Galahad chanced on a little wattled hut with a few wooden or pottery dishes lying about the edge of a clearing. "Donnán," thought Galahad. He knew the hermit had found Kerry too populated, Somerset too close to populated places, and he wondered how long he would stay here. At least he was again feeding the wild creatures.

Just then Donnán appeared, basket on arm, peering at the huge white horse pawing impatiently before his house. Galahad was alarmed at his appearance. He had been old, of course, but very active and full of mischief in Camelot. Now his eyes were sunken, his skin almost transparent, and the tufts of gray hair that more or less outlined his peculiar tonsure had almost completely vanished. He coughed frequently, a hard wracking cough.

Galahad knew instinctively that Donnán would not want coddling and that he probably knew better than anyone how very ill he was. He greeted him with the warm friendship he felt, suppressing the alarm. "Father, I have shield as well as sword now."

Donnán beamed and coughed. His voice was hoarse and difficult to follow. "A brave lad! It's astounded they were at Pentecost. But be so good, it's the wee folk are wanting their evening bits. Could ye spread them? That's the lad." He went off into a fit of coughing that seemed to come from deep in his chest, hard and dry.

Galahad picked up the basket as Donnán set it down and lowered himself to a seat on the stump by his door. First Galahad removed his horse's bridle and substituted a crude halter. Then he led him to the far side of the clearing and tethered him where the grass grew lush. Then he scattered the nuts and berries near the door of the hut. Donnán had gone inside and Galahad found him lying on a mat, his eyes half closed. "There's a wee bit of bread and half a frog the kingfisher deserted. No, yonder by the door."

Galahad took these new offerings outside. Already two squirrels and a jay were looking over the nuts. He set the rest in a dish on the stump and returned inside.

"Ye'd like a bite to eat," said Donnán. Again that deep cough.

"Can I get you something?" Galahad inquired.

"It's little I have. I'm not here long and few folk are minded to me."

Galahad went to the saddle he had left outside and fetched a fresh loaf, a plump cheese, and some cabbage. He also produced a bottle of wine and one of ale. The little man's eyes shone. "It's a feast!" he cried and went off into a long fit of coughing.

As they nibbled away he managed to inquire whether Galahad would need the rest of the loaf and the bottles. Galahad assured him he could find more for himself in the next village and bring back more to Donnán if he wished. "For the little people," said the hermit.

Galahad talked of his adventures since knighthood and of the problems that faced him. When one stumbles on two knights fighting and one is being badly trounced, how do you know

which should be helped? Following without com-
plaint the rules of others is easy, but he came
from country quiet to the court and launched
on a man's work without preliminary preparation in dealing with others. Donnán listened to
him, rarely saying anything. When he did speak
it was in Latin, which he seemed to prefer for
moral counseling.

"Galahad, you have a good heart and you
think true. Men talk a lot of brotherly love without practicing it. You will find men often love
you more for seeing less of you, and in the main
you will love them more if you stand aloof." At
this point he again choked, and coughed until
his face was gray. Galahad offered more wine,
and after a sip or two Donnán resumed, but
Galahad interrupted: "No, father, it wearies you.
Let us talk in the morning."

The old man smiled and said in British:
"In the morning is it? Nay, lad, there is so much
to say. Have you heard that your mother is
dead?"

Galahad had not heard and he gasped –
almost a sob, and the tears stung his eyes. He
was surprised and felt as in a dream when a
part of him seemed to be looking on an expres-
sion of emotion – exaggerated emotion – that
he had not expected. The parting at Joyeux Gard
had been totally unemotional on both sides.

"There, my lad," comforted Donnán, "it
is in great pain was your mother at the end – a
return of the old evils for her tormenting like
those years before your father came to her.

Death was a happy release from a miserable life."

In a choked voice the young knight blurted out: "It's not for her death but her life I'm miserable. She knew so little joy."

"Ay, lad, indeed," Donnán replied. "But joy and misery are of our own making." He had lapsed back into Latin, and spoke softly in a hoarse voice, often pausing for a paroxysm of coughing. "When your father left your mother, she might have turned to you for the warmth and solace your father could not and would not give. But instead – and luckily for you – she turned to the church. Your grandfather, King Pelles, loved her and had heen in torment because of her unhappiness, but she left him in Castle Corbin and stayed at Joyeux Gard. She would accept happiness – love – only on her terms: Lancelot or nothing.

"Perhaps even her misery was a kind of happiness. Remember we all make terms with life as we must. She chose her way, and with her physical wretchedness added to her mental torment, the church she loved, the other life she longed for, were her only road to peace."

During the fit of coughing that followed, Galahad's grief diminished. "Father," said he, "you do not offer the comfort Father Peter would."

Donnán's coughing became indistinguishable from a chuckle. "No," he continued, "I suppose not. He would tell you of the joys of heaven and picture your mother in rapture, contemplating the Deity and singing Hallelujah and Hosanna with the choir of angels. She would like that." He coughed once more as Galahad, beginning to smile, acknowledged the truth of the account.

"Father Peter is of a family that goes back to Rome. They came with the army and various ones in his direct line have been priests and teachers. But there was an Irishman – Pelagius, the Romans called him – who taught that man forges his own destiny. Of course Rome pronounced him a heretic, but there is much good in that heresy. He would not have us blame original sin for our short-comings. At every point, he would say, we choose right or wrong – mostly wrong, and perhaps that is the sin. But we choose – as your mother chose – and we engineer our own destinies." He muttered something in Irish that Galahad could not understand. "It is an old verse," he explained, "that tells the Irish to seek God in their own hearts, not in the Roman basilica."

"And my father and the queen?" Galahad asked.

Donnán spoke bluntly as if to get to the point while his breath lasted. "Your father is a fool. I have often wondered how two such different fools could engender so wise a son. Lancelot is a man of integrity and passion. Every day of his life it hurts him that he did not – could not – marry your mother, and every day of his life it hurts him that he so loves the queen, wife of the man he admires most in all the world

– his friend, his king.

"Now Guenever – she is the wise one. She finds herself loving two men at once. She did not seek it; it stunned her at first. But when she recognized what had happened, she accepted her fate without a backward look. She is intensely loyal to them both. She has never looked at a third, and never will. Where Lancelot grieves for his falseness and feels his life is a living lie, Guenever knows her heart's truth and steadfastness even in its division. You are more like her than like either of your parents, but you are luckier than she. The conflict makes her more uncomfortable, more irascible than you will ever be, but you are equally sensitive to the hearts around you. Be glad, my boy, for the experiences denied you. A happy heart follows unexciting ways."

Galahad wondered if Donnán's second sight had told him of Keren or of Melias, his wayward squire. But he did not ask. The hermit was now choking as if he were coughing up his very lungs, and there were traces of blood on the cloth with which he wiped his lips.

Donnán's thoughts were wandering and when he spoke again he had returned to an earlier thread of the talk so that Galahad took a minute to catch up with his meaning.

"There are a few, not many, of the Round Table who will think as you do that to serve God is to serve oneself, and to help others is to serve God. Do not worry about the ones noisy after drink, loud in challenges and boasting of exploits. Especially, give no time to those whose sole talk is of women. Their accomplishments are rarely half of their claims. Do what you think right. You are blessed with good luck and a contented disposition. Those who love you are those you should love – especially your father. There is a great man of great heart, though not a wise one."

Donnán had hardly got through this speech, and now he coughed without let, ending in a gush of blood. Galahad was frightened, but the old man wagged a finger at him. "Remember that song," he whispered: "'Be it sundown, be it dawn' the last line 'the hour – woe – unknown 'til gone?' I know, I know."

In the morning Donnán was dead. They had said their evening prayers together, not their matins. Galahad scattered the loaf, more nuts, and cheese rinds for the wild creatures, and took the little body across his saddle bow for burial in the village churchyard. When they asked what to put on the cross above him, he could suggest only his name and the year of his death: Sc Donnán, A.D. 560, Requiescat in Pace.

Galahad now turned his horse west toward Powys and then north to where the Conwy pours into the Irish Sea. He turned south again into the mountains where the road was deep in leaves and sheltered from the winds of October. He knew that Dafydd and Caitlin lived in the district, and from Conwy on he was directed toward the lands of Dafydd ap Hoel.

It was late afternoon when he arrived at

the gate and was let in by a stooped gray-haired churl who at once dispatched his long-legged grandson to ride ahead and let the lady of the house know a visitor was approaching. Galahad let his destrier plod slowly after, but the boy had cut straight across fences, hedges and hills and would doubtless have been there first without favors. He dismounted before the large house and gave the groom his horse. As he turned away, Caitlin was on the doorstep with children all about, the youngest in her arms.

"Oh Cú," she greeted him, "it is your name will be on Britain forever. Tomas, Galahad it is, best knight of the world."

The boy came forward shyly. He had dark brown hair like his father's, not the red shock of the younger children that clung to Caitlin's skirts or around her neck. All the children seemed timid, as children do who meet few strangers. Tomas bowed, however, at the introduction.

"Will you bide the night?" she asked. "Dafydd will be wild mad if you are after coming and he off today in long hunting."

Galahad agreed to stay; his stallion needed a good stall and food and care that were too often missing. Even that one night reinforced in Galahad that the world of the child vanishes, and best so. For Caitlin it was still alive as she must see the world from her children's point of view, but she seemed to have stopped growing at twenty when she married. Her whole concern was with the children; all her songs now seemed lullabies.

Dafydd appeared at last. He had still the kind smile and the pleasant manner, but was heavier now and must look up to Galahad, who had been shorter than Caitlin at the wedding. The wandering minstrel of Joyeux Gard now talked mostly of problems of the little farms or the management of the forests and grazing lands, and the development of the harbor at Conwy. The couple were happily matched, and less trapped by than at home in their domesticity.

Galahad was aware that he was a disappointment to them. He did not come with great tales of adventures and court gossip. He could not make his own feats interesting; success teaches less than defeat and one's own success does not make a good tale. Tomas as the eldest was permitted to stay with the family and their guest after supper. The little ones had been carried off half asleep before Dafydd's return.

"Are you really the best knight in the world?" Tomas suddenly asked. Clearly it was much on his mind.

"Tomas," put in Caitlin, "it's he there's the talk of. Just knighted he was and they seated him in the Siege Perilous, and he a beardless boy."

"It is true they say so," said Galahad, "but Tomas, how would I know? Any knight I unseated would say so. It makes it less of a defeat for him."

"Did you ever meet Lancelot?" Dafydd

continued.

"Yes," he replied.

"Don't stop there, Cú," cried Caitlín.

"Well, he went down, but his lance broke and his horse stumbled all at once."

"It's your mother would be the glad-eyed one that day," laughed Caitlín.

"Why?" asked the boy.

"Surely," interrupted Dafydd, "you must know Lancelot was the best knight in the world, and wouldn't any mother want her son to topple him?"

"So," thought Galahad, "they have not told the boy all the gossip."

"Then you have to be the best knight in the world," persisted Tomas.

"I'm playing at it," laughed Galahad, "just don't tell them about the flawed lance and the beast of a horse he was riding."

On his way south through Wales Galahad came on an adventure that was to prove him, yet again, the best of the knights of the Round Table. He had approached a castle where there was a tourney in progress. But it was an especially bloody fight to be just in fun, and those of the castle were pushed back within the gates, and those nearest the gates were being assaulted and killed as the attackers pleased.

Sir Gawaine and Sir Ector de Maris were in the attacking party and saw Galahad ride up. They recognized the red cross on the white shield as well as his red trappings, and they thought it prudent to keep out of his way. He, however, rushed in to help the weaker side without glancing at the opposing forces. His lance broke in the first assault and he was furiously swinging his sword. Not able to see well through the visor and heading for those most sorely pressed, he bore down on Gawaine and brought that shining blade he had drawn from the stone full on Gawaine's helmet. It cut through the metal and deep into the leather cap below, straight to the bone. As the point slipped back as the horses plunged, Gawaine's horse too was badly wounded.

Galahad especially disliked injuring animals. He had no quarrel with them, and felt he could hardly be doing God's work when the beasts suffered. By now the tide of battle had clearly been turned, and off he rode.

Sir Ector was Lancelot's cousin and under no circumstances would attack his son. He had, therefore, withdrawn when Gawaine fell, but now hurried to his side.

"Help me," Gawaine groaned. "They said that sword would wound those who tried to draw it unworthily."

"Yes," said Ector to comfort him, "and I hear Percival has had his blow, and has survived. May you too. Meanwhile the boy has disappeared. Let us make our peace at the castle and find you a leech there."

Chapter IX

Fellowship

Ware thee from the bere prey, avantir last he bite,
For seld he stintit of his pley bot yif he bite or smite

Harley ms. 7322

Thereafter was my vision yet more keen
than was our speech, that fails at such a sight
and memory fades at such glory seen.
As he who dreams and when the dream takes flight
the stamped impression lingers in his thought,
his mind recalls naught else nor sees aright;
Yet such am I - the vision that I sought
now all but lost, yet still its sweetness fills
my heart - the essence of the rapture caught.

Dante, *Paradiso* xxxiii.55ff

Three years of quest had drawn to a close, and at Easter of the following year Galahad turned south toward Camelot. He knew in his heart that the city would not show the glad spring of his first visit, but though he felt alien to it, yet it was now the only home he would claim. Let his father have Joyeux Gard. That had been his childhood, his preparation; it was not the world.

Hedges were white or pink with blossoms; new green leaves fringed the trees and the dawnlight shining through the morning mists rising from the river illuminated globes of new yellowgreen leaves on alder against the boles of lichengray elms and oaks. The dew spangled the branches in the light and a chiffchaff called his drip-drop notes from the tall trees. In open country the budded tips of gorse and broom shone yellow against the dark foliage that cloaked the hillslopes. Hedgesparrows, chaffinches, and yellowhammers twittered and sang. Cuckoos, throstles and blackbirds joined in, piping the young man into Camelot.

On the day Galahad at last reached Arthur's keep, the shadows were long on the grass and the townsfolk sat about enjoying the end of a fine day, soon to go to bed. Galahad entered the keep only briefly to leave his armor, then returned to the stable to make sure his destrier was properly fed and groomed.

As he returned to the hall where the unmarried knights slept on benches, he saw

Lancelot in the courtyard with another knight. They were laughing at something. Then as Lancelot turned toward the living quarters, he clapped his hand on the shoulder of the other in farewell. The other then turned and came toward Galahad, who had paused out of curiosity. It was Gareth, Gawaine's younger brother.

They greeted each other happily. "Have you eaten yet?" asked Gareth. Galahad admitted that he had not and they went off together to the kitchen to see if anything could be found. A surly boy gave them mugs of ale, and to Galahad bread and cheese and a bowl of soup, still warm in the big iron kettle suspended over the banked fire where it would stay warm without cooking until next day.

They asked how each other had fared, and mentioned a few of their encounters. Galahad told of King Bagdemagus and the shield, and of Gawaine's slaughter of the knights Galahad had refused to pursue.

"Yes, my brother is like that," said Gareth. "He seems angry with the world, and hates to be bested, or to leave work half done. That is the best and the worst of him. I hear, too, that you actually unseated Lancelot."

"Oh, not really," said the younger. "His horse stumbled and his lance snapped. Who told you?"

"He did, of course. He said you tossed him fairly, and he laughed as if he had liked it, but he must have been surprised. I wish you had met my brother."

"That happened, too."

"Now there's a difference. He was back a month and never mentioned it – wounded, too. He had a nasty gash on his head, newly healed when he came." He paused and looked at Galahad quizically. "Were you the one who gave it?"

Galahad nodded and told him of the confusion of the encounter.

"Perhaps he didn't recognize you," said the brother.

"He knew the sword. It was the one he had tried to draw from the stone."

"Oh, yes, like Percivale. But Percivale and Lancelot came back together telling everyone about you."

Galahad could see that Gareth cared more for these two than for his brothers. The brothers were inclined to be morose and quarrelsome. The others had equal courage, but though they never tried to avoid a combat, they never provoked one. Galahad thought, "Gareth is more like my father than like his own family. They are like father and son, except for their ages."

Galahad was now in his early twenties, Gareth some ten years older, and Lancelot in his early forties, just Gawaine's age.

"Is Percivale here?" Galahad asked.

"Oh no, he came back with Lancelot after the slash you gave him, but they have been off again, and Lancelot returned a second time only about two nights ago."

The meal, such as it was, was ended and the dark was setting in. A nightingale saluted the last streaks of light in the west and the half moon was high in the sky. As they came out of the kitchen, a figure appeared from the shadows and joined them.

"Good evening, brother," said the shadow.

"Oh, Mordred, I couldn't recognize you in the dark."

"And this is our boy wonder back again? Fellow bastard, we have much in common."

Galahad knew very little of court gossip, but since everyone there thought of little else, they assumed he was informed and told him nothing. He could have asked, but he felt that if it were a concern of his, he would know, and if no concern of his it was a waste of breath.

"Galahad, we have much in common," pursued Mordred, "but at least my father takes me into fosterage and announces me as his heir. Yours might do as much for you."

"Unacknowledged, one can make one's own way," said Galahad softly.

"But the fun you might have," persisted the other. "How you could needle him before the Queen with your claims, news of your mother, shows of affection."

"My mother is dead," Galahad replied.

"Alas, how sad," Mordred remarked casually. "I wish I could say as much for mine."

"Come, now," put in Gareth, "she may have faults, but she is devoted to you. She always made clear you were better born than we and indulged you over all four of Lot's sons."

"I'm tired," said Galahad. "Let's talk in the morning."

They went into the hall, stripped off their clothes, and rolled in blankets on the benches along the walls.

The next morning Galahad joined others in audience with the King to pay him his respects. Only a small portion of Arthur's company was there, and the meeting was informal. Those with grievances were assigned to some official to look into their complaints. Reports from such officials assigned earlier brought either dismissal of the suit or appropriate justice. Finally the knights of the Round Table, recently returned,came forward to be recognized, Galahad among them.

"We have heard something of your exploits, Galahad," said the King. "There are a few aching heads back here to your credit. But how do you find matters throughout the realm?"

"There are good and bad men everywhere, your majesty," the youth replied. "Sin has delight for some, and I foresee no great change. But of yourself and your court and your administration, I heard only admiring words. The country is stronger and more united now than ever in the past."

"Good," said Arthur, obviously pleased, "but I could wish that sin had not penetrated the court so thoroughly."

"But, my lord," said the young man, "it seems to me that without that, the people might admire you more but love you less. Sin has its uses or God would not have put it on earth. There is all eternity to enjoy the perfect world."

Arthur looked at him with an amused smile. "That is strange speech for one who has been acclaimed free of worldly sin and who has sat in the Siege Perilous unscathed. Even with so little experience of this world, perhaps you see more clearly than the rest of us."

The King looked hard at the boy with the look Lancelot had given him when his name was revealed on the Siege Perilous. It was as if he were thinking, "If only I had such a son!"

Arthur turned now to another matter. "There is a lesser task we would enlist you for. May it give you a diversion. A beast – quite a marvelous one could we credit all the tales of it – has been ravaging the woodlands north and west of here. Perhaps you would go along with a dozen or so others and hunt it down. The serfs are in terror, the flocks and herds endangered and so many fine hounds have been ripped to pieces that the region has turned to us for help."

"As you will, my lord," Galahad replied. He withdrew wondering who else would be on this expedition. Lancelot had not been present at the audience; would he take on a mere hunting expedition?

When Galahad next met Gareth he learned that there had already been much talk of this very minor operation. Seemingly it would be for the younger men in hunting clothes on light, swift horses. They would set out in two days' time, take two days riding to get to the afflicted region, and work out a strategy where they could learn something practical about the beast's habits.

The two days before were spent in selecting appropriate steeds and equipment – swords, of course, knives, wooden maces with knotted, knobbed heads in the expectation that the creature would turn iron weapons. It was rumored to have horny armor or thick hair or magic spells. Nothing consistent could be learned from the fantasies of frightened men and women, but perhaps they might see its spoor.

Galahad was more curious than eager. Gareth was excited, for he had found Camelot dull in the weeks since his last excursion. Mordred would be there, too. He said he looked on it as his duty to help Galahad to be a proper bastard.

Agravaine, the most surly of Gareth's brothers, was the oldest and therefore the leader. Mordred suddenly became very deferential to his half-brother, and was maneuvering himself so well into a position of command, or at least consultation, that he troubled very little with Gareth and Galahad.

The first afternoon Gareth remarked, "Lancelot asked me to go with him to the armorer 's. Would you like to come along?"

Galahad thought, "Should I? But he could have asked me, if he chose."

"No," he replied, "I think I'll look over the new hunters that the groom thought would arrive today. If that doesn't take too long, I'll get there later, or perhaps tomorrow."

The new mounts proved to be of excellent quality. They were all a bit nervous in the new quarters with the huge steeds for the armored men. Galahad's white stallion was only moderately interested in his master, wary, perhaps, lest they leave these comfortable quarters too soon again.

Galahad inquired of the stable boy if he had had any exercise that day. "Oh, ay, marster," the boy drawled. "'E 'as been aout for a gude trot abaout the tourney field. 'E do 'ave speerit for zo big 'un."

Turning then to the new lot, Galahad selected a bay mare that reminded him of Kate, whom he had ridden so long ago in a world remote and never to be seen again. When he left the stables only about an hour and a half had passed, so he turned toward the armorer 's.

Weapons and armor of every kind covered the walls of the little shop in the town, and Lancelot and Gareth were still there discussing repairs that had been made, and were yet to be made, and bargaining for replacements. Lancelot had but recently returned and the beaver of his helmet had been damaged by the glancing thrust of a lance. His swordblade, too, had snapped. They went over the weapons and armor carefully, like women shopping for clothes, noting materials and workmanship, relishing the examples of fine ornamentation, and testing the weight and balance.

At first Galahad thought not to disturb them, but they had turned to the lighter weapons to equip Gareth, just the pieces Galahad himself had come for. Lancelot gave him a warm greeting and advised the two younger men on their choices. They would need a light sword, chiefly for thrusting, but with a useful edge if the need arose, and besides a shorter blade, a dagger or long knife, if they were cornered by the beast, and for cutting up the creature if they succeeded in killing it. Galahad caught sight of a blade that took his fancy. It was apparently of Irish workmanship with curling horns on the hilt, a very short crossbar between blade and heft, and about four inches of scrollwork along the thick of the wide blade. It would do excellently, he thought, for the shorter weapon, with a long, light thrusting blade for the other, probably a French weapon. Lancelot thought perhaps a narrower blade would be more useful for the dagger, but when he saw Galahad return to it after trying several other blades and finding fault with each, he laughed and said, "Take it, lad, a man's weapons are a part of him, and what he chooses himself is always right for him."

The armorer was delighted at all the business and commented on the wise choices. The stock was partly his own make, partly bought from the fighters with weapons plundered after a battle, partly by barter and exchange. He drove a hard bargain, but he could be counted on to point out truthfully any flaws or advantages of his stock. All four were pleased.

They returned to Arthur's fort in the late afternoon, just as the second meal of the day had been prepared. There would be no more meals that day, for it was the custom then to have only two, and those often without meat unless there had been a successful hunt. Knight errantry caused less deprivation than had they been accustomed to three meals or more.

As they arrived at the green before the fort, Lancelot, who had been walking between the boys, dropped back and moved to the further side of Gareth, away from Galahad. As he did so, he glanced up at the tower where were the women's quarters. His manner to Galahad became slightly more formal. "He doesn't want to hurt her," the boy thought, and he realized that his father had doubtless welcomed the accidental meeting on the neutral ground of the armorer's.

The next morning Gareth went off to the stables to pick his own mount. A noisy dispute broke out in the courtyard as Galahad was crossing it. Mordred was holding a lad tightly by the wrist. His other hand held a drawn sword, and an old man was pleading with him.

"He's a thieving rascal," shouted Mordred, his face flushed. "Of course he won't admit he stole it, but where is it, then? I ask you, where is it?"

The old man was weeping. "But marster, 'e's a good boy. 'E tell 'un no law-iz. If 'n 'e zeth 'e a'n't no naw-if, 'e a'tn't. Zee fer zel'."

"You all know the price for stealing," screamed Mordred, brandishing the sword. "It's the loss of a hand."

"But marster, 'e's but a lad, an' a craftsman apprentice. Take a 'and from 'im? Best kill 'im outright."

The boy, who had been struggling and bawling all this time, now sent up even more doleful howls. The dogs began to bark and a little crowd gathered.

It looked as if the audience only excited the knight the more, and any moment he might sever the hand or kill the boy or both. Galahad could stand it no longer and stepped forward and grasped the wrist that held the sword.

"My lord, Mordred," he said, speaking formally to try to appease him, "you must let justice be done after the appropriate manner. It is beneath you to do the work of an executioner."

Mordred turned on him with a sneer, and now he began to struggle to free himself. "Let go of me, you damned bastard. You have assumed too much since the day you first set foot in this court. Unhand me, I say."

"Not until you drop that lad and that sword," insisted Galahad.

"He's nothing but a dirty carpenter's son. Take your hand off me."

"Our Lord Christ chose to be no more," said Galahad, and bent Mordred's wrist until the sword dropped to the ground. Mordred loosed his grip on the boy and started to reach for the sword with the other hand, but Galahad jerked his arm forward at just the moment to throw him off balance, and Mordred went sprawling onto the cobblestones. When he recovered, the boy and his father had disappeared.

"What is the story of the loss?" asked Galahad.

"I hold you responsible. I had him terrified; he soon would have confessed had you not interfered," growled Mordred, and went on as if to prove how stupid interference had been. "I bought a dagger for the hunt yesterday morning. Then I came back here to select a mount. I came back to my room in the sleeping quarters first, and the only other place I went was the carpenter's. He was making me a box to hold my property while I was away – a strong chest it is, rather handsome. That fellow and his thieving son have a delicate hand at ornament. When I got back to my room the dagger was missing, and I remembered I had had it at the cabinetmaker's, for I had tried it on a scrap of the leather he had used for hinges. It was a good sharp blade, not like the end of a hurleystick, like that blade you're carrying."

"Have you looked in the stable?"

"No, I didn't use it there so it was not out of its sheath."

"Well, I wanted to look in on my horses; let us look there."

"I've told you, the boy stole it."

Nevertheless, he followed Galahad to the stable, and there on a ledge they found the knife. "The boy must have been frightened into putting it where I'd find it," was all Mordred said. But any friendship between these two was not furthered by that episode.

Next day a dozen knights and half a dozen squires set out for the northwest. At every inn or tavern where they stopped they heard news of the ravening creature. The only common features of the accounts were that it was large – the size of a horse was the smallest size mentioned. It was fierce and ill-tempered and very dangerous.

By the time they reached the marches of Wales, people spoke of a giant covered with hair that lived in the deep forest, and they were able to see a cow and a man that had been clawed by it, and others who claimed to have seen it. Finally someone offered to show them the track.

Gradually they pieced together a fairly definite picture and guessed that it was a small dragon, a wild man of gigantic proportions, a demon, or a wild beast. Unless it was a totally unknown creature, it must be a bear, though bears had long been unknown except in the Caledonian forest. Then at last they saw the track and knew indeed that it was a bear, perhaps old and ill, driven out of the usual haunts of bear and turning in desperation to the docile cattle and sheep of these less rugged lands.

Galahad was glad to be so near the end of the quest. Mostly he had ridden with Gareth, but Mordred never lost an occasion to sneer at him and always addressed him as "bastard." Mordred's fawning ways of currying favor with

Agravaine might have been annoying, except that it kept him at the head of the troop and Gareth and Galahad brought up the rear – a position that provided Mordred with further barbs.

The little group, less than twenty men in all, used the strategy that might be expected of Agravaine, that is, a direct confrontation without strategy. It was difficult to find beaters among the terrified men of the region, but the local lords were only too eager to offer the lives of their serfs and freemen, and set such tempting rewards that they found men to risk their lives for it.

The group of mounted knights, backed up by the squires, waited between a bank of rocks with rolling gravel and the river. Agravaine was in the center, Mordred and Galahad to his right, Gareth and Gereint to his left. The other seven knights were young and untried and had come hoping to prove themselves worthy of the brotherhood of the Round Table. Behind them were the squires, who had brought the pack horses and were armed with bows and arrows. From the other side of the slope the beaters moved slowly, shouting as they came. No dogs were used, for the beast had shown itself quite capable of dealing with them singly or in packs, and was more likely to be startled by the men. Although word had it that the woods and a shallow cave were its present area of operation, there was always a chance there would be no quarry when the beaters finally made their way to the narrow ravine where the knights waited, horses growing more nervous by the moment as they sensed the tenseness of their riders.

Mordred regretted having persuaded his brother to make him second in command. He had suggested perhaps the beaters would need someone to guide them, but Agravaine, who could not imagine anyone's not wanting the excitement of the point of danger, wouldn't hear of the sacrifice.

The beaters did not move rapidly and it was over an hour before their shouts could be heard by the knights. On the other hand, the beast was alarmed at those distant sounds and unaware of the ambush, for the wind was in the north, blowing toward the waiting company. It was almost on them before it realized their presence, and the danger of its position. They saw a thicket move, heard a growl of surprise, and not long after the scream of a beater as the beast tried to get through the pack coming from behind. The mob was larger and noisier than the little company of men, and it made no further pursuit, but doubled back toward the south.

The beaters moved cautiously now, aware that the beast was indeed nearby, and for a while all was still except for the clamor of the slowly advancing beaters. The bear, at last broke from cover, snarling and growling. Horses neighed in terror, and Agravaine spurred forward with sword drawn. Had the bear tried to climb the slope, it would have been slowed by shifting gravel, and had it plunged into the river, it would have been an equally easy target for the archers. But Agravaine's approach concentrated the attack and with a roar, the bear struck at his horse. Agravaine was quick to respond, but his thrust was shaken by his plunging steed, and the blade snapped off in the bear's shoulder. Cornered and wounded it exhibited a fury that had been the foundation of the terrified tales of giants, magic power, and dragons.

As the bear turned now toward the river, the nearest rider was Mordred, who was pale with terror. The beast gashed his horse which in turn screamed and reared, and Mordred had all he could do to keep his seat, without drawing his sword. He tried to turn his horse even as the bear was clawing at it, and in his misery he too screamed. Galahad spurred the bay quickly forward, interposing himself between the enfuriated bear and the terrified Mordred. The slim point of his French sword he thrust at the bear, striking at the base of its throat and plunging to his heart. The poor beast gurgled, slumped forward, and died in one last violent convulsion.

Galahad all but lost his balance, but he had chosen his mount well, and she stood firm, trembling, but well under control. Mordred turned his bleeding horse about and clearly fled. Agravaine's horse was injured also, and the knights now dismounted to carve up the bear. The claws, head, and skin would be taken to Arthur, the meat smoked, then roasted for the villagers, the choice hindquarters going to the family of the beater who had been killed.

Agravaine had offered Galahad the honor of skinning and disemboweling the bear, but Galahad declined. As leader, Agravaine could rightly have claimed the privilege, and Galahad saw by the alacrity of his acceptance that he was eager for the opportunity. The dressing of the quarry was an important ritual in those days, and Galahad, who shunned hunting for sport, knew well that he could not execute the task with the expertise and the flourish of Agravaine. Besides the very thought of it was distasteful to him.

As Agravaine worked, Gareth complimented Galahad on his diplomacy, and continued, "How did you act so quickly? You hate hunting, and yet you dispatched it more neatly than any of us could have done."

"I went on this adventure; I could have stayed had I wished. There can be mercy, too, in a quick, clean kill. That poor old beast against so many might have died by inches."

Agravaine commended Galahad's skill and offered him the head. Galahad would not accept, but bade him take all the trophies to King Arthur.

After that Mordred ceased to call Galahad "bastard," nor did he speak of him by name, but resorted to the earlier title "boy wonder."

When the successful troop trotted into Camelot with their spoils, laden with gifts from the grateful folk of the west country, they found

Sir Percivale there before them. Galahad winced at the red scar curving down from his hair across his forehead. But his cousin welcomed him warmly, and Gareth and the other two became inseparable. Mordred kept aloof, abandoning the bachelor's quarters in the hall for the more comfortable rooms of Arthur's tower.

One lack in the companionship between Gareth and Galahad was their differences in religious observance and religious feeling. The sons of Morgause, Queen of Orkney, all took their religion lightly. The three oldest – Gawaine, Agravaine, and Gaheris – rarely attended chapel except at high feasts, and Mordred openly made fun of religion, though he attended more regularly, as if to ingratiate himself with the King's household. He could make a grave show of piety and confession before matins and utter the direst blasphemies after nones, calling the Lord Jesus a bastard like himself.

All the brothers except Gareth laughed at Galahad, and Gareth was too honest to pretend that religion was one of his prime concerns. With the coming of Percivale, Galahad suddenly could talk of aspects of his adventures about which he had been silent before.

One evening Galahad and Percivale sat talking as twilight deepened and nightbirds began joining in the last chorus of the day. Gareth was elsewhere with Lancelot. Galahad could not associate Percivale with the young beardless lad who had looked so old to him then, not much short of twenty years before at Joyeux Gard. At that time Percivale's curling hair and long curling lashes had given him a girl's beauty. Yet now, bearded and heavier, he seemed to Galahad nearer his own age.

Moreover, he asked questions of the younger man as if he were his equal or superior. He was a kind, unassuming, and perpetually innocent knight.

"I am puzzled," he said, "to know the right road. Some time back I was at a strange castle. There was a wounded knight with all the lands about lying waste. They gave me entertainment, and various wonders appeared. Priests have always asked me not to question so much and to accept whatever happens. I was deeply curious, but I dared not ask explanations of my host. They kept me that night, and next day met me weeping, saying that the lord would have been healed and the countryside would have bloomed had I only asked. I have felt guilty ever since."

"Be of good cheer," said Galahad. "God always lets us know when a curse should be lifted. Perhaps the time was not right, or you were not the destined healer."

"Nevertheless," Percivale replied, "I felt I was walking through a folktale with two conflicting instructions: do not ask questions of your host; do ask about mysteries."

"That is why I find religion such a comfort," said Galahad. "If you are troubled about your own conduct, you can go for guidance to confession. If you sin, you can do penance. When things go well, you can express your gratitude and your praise in prayer. The rituals, festivals, rules of conduct are all prescribed. One need not doubt or apologize. My mother gave me no advice or direction. Only the priest could I count on for explanations and for pointing the way."

"More and more I too feel that the only comfort for me is in the church, yet not as a monk or friar or priest, but as one who has business elsewhere, but comes home at nightfall."

Out of that evening a certain restlessness fell on Galahad, an overpowering feeling that he must press on and complete as much as he could of his destined duties. Two days later he again sought an audience with Arthur, explaining why he must go. Again the King gave him a friendly greeting and blessed him and bade him goodbye when he had heard his hopes.

So into the spring with the gorse gilding the hillsides, Galahad rode off on his white stallion. Gareth and Percivale watched him go, each thinking, "Soon I shall follow."

The third evening after he left Camelot, Galahad stopped for the night in a quiet glade where a stream, edged with yellow flags, and daffodils flowed smoothly toward the Thames to the north. The destrier, free of saddle and bridle, had rolled in the grass and now was grazing nearby in the lush meadow while Galahad, his armor piled at the foot of a tree, sat on a log, groping in his scrip for the bread and cheese he had bought at a farmhouse.

He heard a slight rustle in the leaves behind him, and turned just in time to see an
adder lunge at him. Galahad was familiar with
adders and other snakes from his woodland
walks near Joyeux Gard, but he had never before seen one strike – but then, he had usually
seen them first, and had let them go their way.
To his surprise, he felt no sharp pains. The
snake was now coiling back on itself and re-
treating into the shadows, and the knight saw
then that it had struck the broad Celtic blade
that he had bought for the bear-hunt. The serpentine pattern tracing its center ended in a
triangular head like the adder's. He had been
about to draw the knife to cut his cheese. In
another moment his hand or his hip, clad only
in the light jerkin with its leather padded shoulders that he wore below his armor, would have
been exposed to the fangs. "The blade is lucky
for me," he thought. Certainly he had not used
it on the hunt. It might have been useful had
he carved the bear. But Mordred had laughed
at its shape and Lancelot had doubted its usefulness. At least the breadth of blade had helped
him now.

As he turned it over in his hands he
caught sight of a handsome piece of pale redbrown agate by his foot. He had to dig it from
the soil, for only a bit of it showed. What he
found in his hand was a flint blade, not unlike
the Celtic knife in its proportions, but without
a design, and with a waving border where neat
chips had been flaked out of it to sharpen it. He

looked from one to the other and thought back to that day of discovery in his boyhood, the ferret, the chattering brook, the lake, the stone with the rude cross. What was it Donnán had said? "There is no escaping the past. We all come from pagans and sunworshipers like those that raised those stones." He recalled, too, that the kindly hermit had told him of an adder that lived near him and sometimes drank the milk he set out for the little foxes or the wild swine. His own drink tonight was springwater, but he left crumbs of bread and cheese on a rock as an offering to the wild creatures.

It was not yet dark – for it was now May – when he fell asleep on a leafy bed below a sycamore. But he dreamed that he rode his white steed along a shore where wavelets, bright in the moonlight, chased each other forward to the sand, toppling over as they reached the shallows, gleaming and phosphorescent all along the strand. He turned the great horse toward them, and he trotted smoothly out across the waters, hooves sending up little showers like sparks, and the land receding behind them. All before was white mist aglow in the moonlight – no, aglow like a shining cloud and there were arms and eyes beckoning. The land was gone, the heavens opening like great pillared gates on the horizon, and he and the stallion trotting smoothly on and on toward that shining glory.

But the ripples about the stallion's glistening hooves were dark and twisting coils – like the adder, like the patterned blade – and the steed plodded slower, encumbered, shackled in the loops and coils of the molten sea. Galahad felt a great ache, yearning to go forward, but held back by the serpentine waters. Then it was the fetters on his own ankles that were holding him, gray, twisted, shimmering ropes.

In an anguish of yearning he awakened to see the dawnlight glittering through the trees, each drop of dew a spark, and mist rising from the damp ground, catching the rising sun in an aureate glory like the welcoming gates of his dream. Whether it was haste to get the dream from his thoughts or intention to turn from pagan objects, or chance, he did not think of the knives of iron and flint until noon of the day. Donnán had told him his way was toward Christ, toward the east. "I must get away from Eng-land," he thought. But the way to one's destiny cannot be hurried, and his trail was to be a coiling serpentine path.

Chapter X

The Holy Grail

Swete Jesu, well may him be
That thee may in blisse see.
With love-cordes drawe thou me
That I may comen and wone with thee.

Swete Jesu, hevene king,
Feir & best of alle thing,
Thou bring me of this longing
To come to thee at min ending.

Swete Jesu, all folkes reed,
Graunte us er we buen ded
Thee underfonge in fourme of bred,
And sethe to heovene thou us led.

Middle English lyric

bout this time Galahad began having strange, haunting dreams. He
never knew what induced them – perhaps long riding and the scanty
meals, often not more than one a day
and that no more than herbs and berries with
water to drink, or some hermit's offer of bread
and milk. He tasted no meat at all, though once
in a while he was offered fish from a stream.

The dreams came by night or day, for he
often lay for a time at noon, letting his destrier
graze. He could scarcely tell these dreams from
waking. He seemed to board a ship that had no
crew and yet seemed to move myteriously to far-
off lands, the Middle Sea, the outer isles, the
Holy Land. On these ships were letters telling
the history of old swords and jeweled scabbards,
or of beds where holy men had died. The real
world, Camelot, Joyeux Gard, grew ever more
distant, more unfamiliar, more unreal, and he
less content than ever to ride forth blindly,
charging at every armed figure he encountered.

In this half-waking, half-dream world
Galahad met with Bors and Percivale and with
them entered the Castle of Carbonek. Galahad's
grandfather, King Pelles, was there and made
them welcome, but only the three friends and
other threes from Gaul, Denmark, and Ireland
were permitted to behold the rites of the Holy
Grail. Except for the sacred vessel and the
bleeding lance, the rites made visible the miracle
of the sacraments as the form of a child with
brightly glowing contenance seemed to plunge

into the sacramental bread and disappear within it. Then from the housel wine issued the form of a man with the marks of the passion bleeding before them. The dish that held the bread and wine was that that had held the Paschal lamb on Sher-Thursday. The man assured them they would all see it yet more plainly in Sarras, the Holy City. With the bleeding lance, Galahad healed King Pelles, who these many years had suffered from a painful and incapacitating wound.

The mystery, the awe, the intoxicating fragrance, with all that one could desire of music, of food, of beauty, raised the three friends to an ecstasy like dreams from poppy or lotus. But they felt only exaltation, never despair or loss. It came to them as the perfect fulfillment, perfect joy. The brotherhood established by this banquet, by the sharing of this most special blessing, bound Bors, Percival, and Galahad closer than any family ties. They had together experienced the ineffable. Here was the seal of friendship.

But they had other reasons for finding each other the perfect comrades. Bors had had the most normal childhood of the three, for he was cousin to Sir Lancelot. But Percivale had been brought up with an over- protective mother. She paid him much more attention than had Elaine to Galahad, but both had felt the isolation from the excitement – and the vices – of the court. This background, and the visions they had shared, the ideals they believed in, kept these three apart from all other men, even their brothers.

When Galahad found Bors and Percivale on a ship he had entered almost by chance, the joy was mutual. In addition, a nun who was there, assisting in serving them and looking after the younger servants, revealed herself as Percivale's sister. She was much older, actually old enough to be his mother herself. Their mother's fierce protectiveness of her youngest had partly come about because Percivale was a late child, sure to be her last and she wished to keep him forever a child.

The sister was quiet and sensible, and as if she, too, had stepped from Galahad's dreams, she knew many stories of wonders, some of them involving a sword, scabbard, and bed here on the ship. Indeed, she claimed to have made the girdles to support the scabbard chiefly from her own hair, which she had cut on entering the order. Galahad thought of those beautiful braids of Guenever, that she sometimes caught into her girdle. Percivale's hair was thick and curly, almost black; the sister's must have been similar. She insisted that Galahad take the sword. The others joined in her plea, and he recognized that they all believed, as did many whom he met, that he was the knight of destiny. "Dear Lord," he breathed, "let me take this, not as deserving, but for the comfort it will bring them. In Thy love is my strength."

Not long after this the ship came to land not far from Caerliwelydd near the Scottish border. The friends were puzzled how to proceed for, of course, they no longer had their horses, and no one can walk far in full armor. They could see people shouting and gesturing and a girl screamed to them, "Watch out, death lies in your path!" Almost at once they were attacked from a coastal stronghold nearby and surrounded by mounted knights. The three stood back to back and promptly struck down the first three to attack, then grasping the reins of the horses, they mounted before the next wave of warriors closed in on them. Now they could themselves launch an attack and soon they galloped into the castle after the fleeing men, leaving them in pools of blood on the floor.

Bors and Percivale were exultant, but Galahad, who intensely disliked the slaughter, could see little justification for the massacre of men whose only fault seemed to be their having attacked unprovoked. He was close to nausea at the carnage. At that point an old man came from an inner room, looking in bewilderment at the blood and bodies. The three at once knelt before him, helms on their hips. Sir Bors explained that they were knights of Arthur's court, and Percivale added an account of the combat. Galahad spoke last: "Sir, I much repent this killing. As Christian knights they deserved better."

But the hermit would listen to no apologies; he called it rather an "almsdeed" that they were slain, and he proceeded to tell of their rape, murder, and other violent acts. "If it be God's

will, then I am less downcast," Galahad murmured. Then at the old man's invitation he gave
comfort to the imprisoned lord, whom the hermit had been tending. As he bent over the lord,
the sick man thanked God he had been avenged,
but died there with Galahad's arm around him.

Galahad, scarcely reassured after the
slaughter of the knights, now was shaken, but he
could see that indeed the lord had died comforted.
"That," he thought, "is the merit of this glory. If
they believe in me, it lifts their hearts. Thank God
I can yet do something for their peace of mind
when physical help fails."

The four now set out through the
Caledonian Forest. It was dark and wild with tum-
bling streams and the foliage above them shut-
ting out the day. The disorientation that had before troubled Galahad afflicted him worse in the
halfday of these woodlands. Mysteries were revealed in the changing shapes of animals they met,
but the beasts to him were like the illustrations
he had seen in those great vellum Scriptures, the
treasures of their churches. The man and lion
and eagle and ox that they met were more like the
forepages of the Gospels than like creatures of
earth. They and the splendid white stag, Christ
risen, haunted him in the dark hours as his
body lay shaken by chills and fever. Bathed in
perspiration, his head and whole body aching,
he remembered the tales of his mother's afflic-
tion.

Both his physical and mental turmoil was
intermittent. He had a good grasp of reality

when they entered the castle that demanded the bleeding of Percivale's sister. The three friends had refused to yield her up and had defended her, fighting back to back as was their wont. But at day's end they were persuaded to rest there. They never understood just why those they had fought were chosen for defeat and death. For now it was explained to them that only the blood of a clean maiden might heal the lady who lay ill there. The sister then rose and said, "Gladly will I submit to you my blood for so good a cause." She would not look at her brother or his friends, but went quickly from them.

When they found her again, she was deathly pale, even though the lady by her, who had been anointed with her blood, was now sitting up and looking about. They gathered up the sister and staunched her bleeding, but they could see she was near dèath. She asked in a barely audible voice to be set afloat in a barge, and promised that they would again see her and be buried with her. For the time being she asked them to separate until they should meet again at Sarras. After her death, Percivale, weeping, wrote down these adventures as she had told them or as they had happened, and he placed the scroll in her hand as she lay in the barge. Then the three knelt to offer up a prayer for her, and she was carried out to sea on the tide.

That night there arose a wild storm during which a wounded knight appeared. Bors asked for this adventure and the others granted it to him. But all that night they prayed in the chapel for his success. In the morning light they found the graves of all the maidens who had been bled uselessly. "How do I know," thought Galahad, "that the blood I have spilt has been more usefully spilt than theirs?'" But the scene of all those graves recalled the loss of Percivale's sister and her dying command that they separate. With real warmth of feeling Percival and Galahad embraced. Both lonely boys had found at last a comrade in hopes, and in virtue. Nevertheless, as the sister had asked, they parted.

Lancelot could never give a clear account of what happened – obedience to a dream was all he would hint at. But he was the first to enter the barge after Percivale's sister had been sent out to sea. The letter in her hand helped him to reconstruct the adventures. Percivale, Bors, and his son seemed to have been present. He was not surprised then when Galahad came riding up along the shore.

When father and son recognized each other, it was Lancelot who first knelt and asked his son's blessing, In that moment Galahad felt what it was to be the best knight of the world. Here Malory tells only this:

> So dwelled Lancelot and Galahad within that ship half a year, and served God daily and nightly with all their power. And often they arrived in isles far from folk, where there repaired none but wild beasts; and there they

found many strange adventures and perilous, which they brought to an end. But because the adventures were with wild beasts, and not in the quest of the Sancgreal, therefore the tale maketh here no mention thereof, for it would be too long to tell of all those adventures that befell them.

This meeting with his father was like a tonic to the boy. He seemed to gain strength daily, and as his mother had found respite from suffering as soon as Lancelot held out his hand to her, the son too ceased from chills, pain, and fever, and dreams no longer crowded upon him, more real than the ship where he and his father rode. For each it was an island of understanding where for six months past, present, and future were clarified to them. But in other respects this halfyear was like the dreams he had had. Food and drink came miraculously to them and Percivale's sister, as if softly sleeping, lay unchanged in the cabin – or was it her spirit that was with them – pure, serene, willing to sacrifice herself for others?

Life on that ship was an oasis in a world of frustration. Father and son would wake at dawn, light slanting through the mists of the reach where the vessel swung at anchor, strange trees holding a sandbar as tides rose or fell. They watched otters playing – sliding on back or belly down waterslides. The shrieks and chatter of unfamiliar birds broke the silence; a snake or turtle, just its head showing, would trail a V of ripples across the lagoon to better hunting grounds. Deer snorted and withdrew at seeing the ship. Martins and strange ringtailed creatures with sensitive fingers, hunted crawfish in the shallows. Wild cats large and small crossed their path when they wandered inland. At sunset, sky and water glowed red about them as they knelt side by side giving thanks to God for the glory of the world and His all-embracing love.

Lancelot at first when looking on those creatures thought of hunting, but Galahad talked quietly of what he had learned from the Irish hermit, that there is no unlovely beast. They are all God's children and in general they show more loyalty, less ferocity to their own kind than does man. For every bit of bread you take, leave half for the wild creatures, wherever you go. The sparrows and the swine, the deer and rodents, even the ants who are busy ridding the world of its offal, these are all of God and closer to His heart than are those who deny Him.

It pained Galahad that though Lancelot seemed to wish to free himself from his ties to Guenever, though he spoke with unquestionable sincerity of the greatness of Arthur and his àll but divine qualities, that when Galahad suggested he leave Camelot, he said he could not. He paused and put his head in his hands. "My son," he said, "for myself I could give up the world and enter a monastery. But the queen. . . ." He paused and the boy read the struggle in his face. "She loves me as I do her, and she does not find our Lord or the Virgin Mary an adequate replacement. I believe one day, perhaps only after Arthur's death, she will see that there is no guilt, no disappointment, no unfulfillment in that other love. But only then shall I be free."

"You know, father," said Galahad, "once long ago at Joyeux Gard there was a woman. She was deceitful, like my mother; and she was married, like the queen."

"You?" blurted out his father. "The best knight in the world?'"

"I think God watched over me. He made the way smooth for me to fall, but He also gave warnings – that I did not always heed. At last, when I was on the point of asking her to marry me, He sent her husband."

Lancelot spoke very low, "Did your mother know?"

"No," the boy answered. "Mother would have been crushed, especially when my close-ness to God has not seemed to be impaired. But the lesson was to me. I think, father, that I understand you better now, and my mother, and why you would not marry her."

"You may understand these matters better than I do myself."

"The very name of that woman," Galahad continued, "was bitter on my tongue; she had so nearly made a fool of me. As for mother, she never thought of you as a person or saw that a man cannot direct his heart any more than she could hers. But her love for you was real and undying."

"We have each misunderstood the other," said Lancelot.

Galahad also told his father how he had been taught to pray when lonely, as Elaine had done. "I am rarely lonely now," he said. "I grow restless with too much company. But every hour of the day I feel God close to me. My heart is very much at peace."

Father and son would kneel side by side in prayer and for both tranquility would displace all sense of tension. The son observed that though his father always ended his prayers with a prayer for the queen and her happiness, he never mentioned Elaine. So Galahad alone prayed for her and pitied her.

As the ship wandered over the waters on its strange voyage, father and son came to know one another better than most fathers and sons ever can achieve. They shared one kind of isolation, that of being best. Other knights were envious or adulatory. In no way could these two be accepted as fellows among fellows. To deny their superiority would have been more crushing than the simple fact that they were best.

One day Lancelot remarked, "We have talked of the problems of fellowship. Perhaps you see now that King Arthur is the most generous man I know. In the stupid arts of combat he is not the best knight in the world, but in his great ideals, his great understanding of men's hearts, in his utter unselfishness, he is truly great."

Galahad interrupted with the thought

that had long troubled him: "But father – his wife!"

"I think he even guesses that and forgives us. He had arranged the marriage with her father. I doubt that she was ever asked what she wished. Then Arthur left her so far behind she could only honor and respect him, not love him as she should. I was less perfect – much less perfect. Oh, I could sit a horse better, knock down all opponents, but I had neither his vision nor his unselfishness. Had I been less selfish, I might have married your mother."

"Perhaps all this world is hollow," said the son. "What does it hold for Arthur? His nearest and dearest are you, his chief knight, and Guenever – and both have betrayed him."

"Only you could say that to me unharmed'" Lancelot growled.

"But I understand'" cried the boy. "I cannot talk to the knights. What should I say? I do not know the court; I can't talk of what happened years ago; I'm not even interested in it. As for tournaments, so far opponents have crumpled before me as before you. What does one say? The best is a lonely place. Even Guenever – most beautiful, highest in rank – other women use her to raise themselves."

"Have you heard about Mordred's relation to Arthur?" interrupted Lancelot.

"I know nothing about him, but I don't feel drawn to him. He and Arthur are good friends, are they not?"

"Their relationship is somewhat like

yours and mine. Mordred is his son by his half-sister, mother of Gawaine and his brothers. Obviously marriage is out of the question. So runs the gossip. The Welsh, however, say that he is merely Arthur's fosterson. Often enough a sister's son is raised by his uncle."

"But Gawaine and his brothers were not sent to Arthur," put in Galahad.

"That is so, but Mordred was born after Lot's death. Morgause needed a strong defender of the boy – and a father for him."

"What do you believe?"

"I believe Arthur accepted the boy and all the gossip he would bring from family loyalty. Only he knows the truth. If he is innocent, he is still likely to suffer as if he were not."

Galahad was silent a long time. When he spoke his voice was low. "Did Guenever resent this?"

Lancelot thought a moment. "If you mean 'Was she trying to even the score when she turned to me' – no. But I believe Arthur feels he has no right to expect of her a perfection he feels the world thinks he lacks. He gives Mordred every offer of friendship, and loves him as I do you – our only sons. Even if Mordred is his fosterson, he is all the heir Arthur can hope for. But Mordred is more like that adulteress his mother. He despises Arthur; he understands none of his virtue."

"I thought Mordred too old to be Arthur's son."

"Arthur was barely eighteen at the time,

and Morgause has quite a reputation. You have heard of Sir Lamorak?"

"Killed by Agravaine – is that the one?"

"Yes. Of course since Adam we have always blamed the woman, but King Lot's wife had a special brand of beauty and evil. You can see a bit of both in her eldest Gawaine. Yet I find Gawaine straightforward and as close to a comrade as any of Camelot, though I suspect he envies me. His mother was ten or fifteen years older than Arthur when she enchanted him, if he is the father. Mordred was her last child. In her you can see beauty without scruples. Guenever – even Isolt – is so much more worth our admiration."

"So far," said Galahad, thoughtfully, "you have told me only that Guenever is beautiful – which I know – and that she preferred you to Arthur because you are less perfect than he. What is her charm as you see it?'

"My son, you have met her. Is she just a handsome face?"

"No, to be sure. She looks me straight in the eyes. She doesn't treat me as a little boy, as the son she never had. She talks as if I understood the principles of chivalry and the king's ideals. She does not patronize nor caress nor embarrass me."

Lancelot's eyes were shining. "In brief visits you have seen what I love in her. She never detracts from another's dignity by look or word. Even when we have quarreled, she has reproached me only in private. Her conduct has been so carefully guided that no one at court has been able to guess whether or not we were lovers, whether or not we had differences. And that is at the bottom of our sin. I love her so I have not in my heart repented. Even now with you, though I feel this quest is more to me even than she, I cannot promise that I shall give her up. Not if she calls me. I haven't that strength."

"Best of all, if she could renounce you. I think that is what you truly crave."

Lancelot looked off to the horizon where a whale spouted, then breached and sounded. "That would indeed give me my freedom. All heaven to wander through at her side."

"It is still a long road," sighed the son.

One evening Lancelot and Galahad sat watching the moon rise, its silver light snaking across the smooth, subsiding breakers that lisped against the sides of their vessel.

"Father," began the son, "in all the world there will never be a finer knight than you are."

Lancelot grimaced. "Let's not joust with words," he said. "You know the guilt that gnaws at me."

"But father," exclaimed the boy, "don't you see? I don't know guilt. I don't know pain. All my disappointments have been minor. When the world was not to my liking, I could turn my thoughts elsewhere. I was lonely and learned to love being alone. I had always thought that I wanted comrades my own age, but when I met them, I found very few who thought or felt as I did. I never loved any woman enough to break my heart over her. My vanity could be wounded, but that was superficial and inconsequential. I have not even been wounded in combat, but you are a mass of scars. You have courage; even knowing the danger, you can enter contest after contest. I do what I think is right and the way has been made smooth for me. The first time a sword or spear pierced my side I might scream and run. No, father, I am not better than you. That test is forbidden me. This world is beautiful."

The moon was sailing free of clouds now and the shimmering path of light reached across the waters to where the black hull of their vessel interrupted it. A heron flapped homeward; an owl barked.

"But yet," the boy continued, "I would leave all this beauty tomorrow gladly, if it were God's will. My life has a kind of pointlessness. In this world of time and space, change is excitement and reality. I have conquered loneliness by thinking of the eternal, unchanging world. To me that is happiness."

"Yes, my son, we are very unlike," said Lancelot with a sigh. "Each moment of my life I look for a change. Should Guenever love me less, I might turn to the church, but ever I hope she will love me more. My own love, too, can be more intense after absence, less so when hope of heaven occurs to me. This more or less, this now or then, is the world of time and place. I wonder if a man like me could find joy in heaven."

"Oh father, don't say that!" cried the boy. "Heaven is living in the presence of God. One will wish for no change. You and the queen will not need each other. Yet you will have each other in harmony forever."

Lancelot smiled at the boy's eagerness. The boy was wondering and praying, "Will they? Dear God, please let them see heaven."

To the gentle rocking and the waves lapping against the ship's sides and the shore, the men fell asleep.

' On a day at the end of six months they met a knight leading a white horse. It was indeed the stallion that had borne Galahad in his first tournament. It whinnied in delight when it saw him and came trotting up to nuzzle its master. Galahad knew at once that this was a summons over which he had no control. He bade his father farewell, hoping to see him in the next life. Lancelot asked that he pray for him. In the dusk of the forest as they looked at each other they recognized that this was the last time.

"Now, son Galahad," said the older man, "since we shall depart and never see each other more, I pray to the high Father to preserve both you and me."

Galahad knelt as he had knelt to receive the accolade and murmured, "Sire, no prayer avails so much as yours."

Lancelot had   ways felt inferior to this splendid son of his. He lifted him to his feet and embraced him, tears in his eyes. The boy had never reproached him, had never gloated

over him, but had tried to understand him.
Lancelot turned back to the ship and the boy
mounted and disappeared into the forest.

During these days after Galahad's departure from Lancelot, he at first went alone, then
he met with Sir Bors and Sir Percivale. At last
these three, who had more in common with each
other than they had with any other knights, fell
more and more into comradeship. Each of these
three, in differing degrees, was trying to discover himself. The more Galahad felt aware of
the world and his place in it, and the more he
felt assured that God returned the earnest love
he offered, the more he felt detached from the
world. In Bors and Percivale he had companionship and friends who could share and sometimes help him to explain that precarious balance between this world and that other.

The miracles performed in these months
of their companionship were to him all that he
felt he had to offer the world. If men died happier in his arms, he would not deny them that
comfort. The mending of the broken sword of
Joseph of Arimathea he thought was a dream
until he saw Bors weighing the blade approv-
ingly. But he never asked where he got it for
fear of appearing a fool. That was one epithet
he tried not to earn – the one touch of pride in
an essentially humble man. The healing of the
maimed king with the blood of the lance he
thought one of those many miracles that come
with faith. He happened somehow to have the
reputation as the best knight of the world and

a miracleworker. If people earnestly believed that the spirit of God worked through him, then it did work through him because God pitied them.

A lesser man might have taken pride in his humility. Galahad did not. Sincerity and integrity, a natural gentleness and love of God's world were his principal traits. Moreover, he was a generous spirit who wasted no time looking for faults in others, or in himself. Nevertheless, he felt himself lacking in experience – experience he would never acquire.

The three had at last gone to Sarras, the Holy City. As had been predicted, almost at the same time, at least on the same day, the barge bearing the body of Sir Percivale's sister also drifted ashore. Here in this city the friends rested. Although they were briefly cast into prison, the early death of the tyrant freed them, and the citizens proclaimed Galahad their king. He had learned to accept his fate, and without protest he accepted this. He told no one that he was deathly ill. Since he had left his father his condition had steadily deteriorated. His bones ached, his vision was often blurred, his head throbbed and the dreams and disorientation that had afflicted him earlier now haunted him night and day. He relied heavily on Bors and Percivale, but fortunately his duties were chiefly ceremonial. Each morning they prayed at a golden altar that they had had erected, and in his prayers morning and evening, Galahad found moments of peace, moments without physical pain. He longed in his heart to spend the entire day so. How his head ached!

At last the anniversary of his crowning came around. He tried to walk erect, but his friends had seen him falter at the head of the palace steps and had quietly grasped his elbows. Thus steadied, he descended calmly, a gentle smile on his lips. Today would be the formal celebration of a high mass. His ears were ringing, his head swimming. He closed his eyes a moment and beheld Jesus and the twelve apostles, seated at a table where was wine and flat pieces of bread. He saw them eat; he heard them speak.

Galahad was trembling from head to foot. He raised his hands and cried, "Lord, I thank Thee, for now I see this that has been my desire many a day. Now, blessed Lord, would I not longer live, if it might please Thee, Lord." When they offered him the sacrament he accepted with a smile, his eyes fixed on the crucifix behind the table. But what he saw there was the face of Jesus smiling back at him.

He rose unsteadily and went first to Percivale and then to Bors. He clasped their hands and then embraced them in turn, commending them to God. To Bors he also whispered, "Fair lord, salute me to my lord Sir Lancelot, my father, and as soon as ye see him, bid him remember the unstable world." He staggered slightly but disguised it by kneeling to pray. In that prayer he slipped sideways and never rose again.

Percivale died soon after and only Bors again saw Camelot. Only he of the Round Table had seen the Holy Grail and the heavenly city of Sarras and had returned to tell of it.

One hears that Lancelot slid back into the old ways and was banished from the court. He was not then there to aid his king when Mordred rose against him. But when the kingdom fell, Guenever entered a convent. It was with no small joy that Lancelot followed to a monastery, They never met again in life nor in death. For Lancelot insisted that she be buried beside Arthur, not in the convent chapel as the nuns had wished.

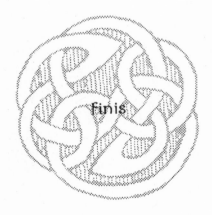

finis

Manuscript sources of early English, Irish, and Welsh poetry quoted in *Blessed Bastard*

Chapter I
"Wolde God that it were so." Ms: Cambridge U.L. Add 5943, folio 164b but in a later hand.

Chapter II
"I must go walk the wood so wild." Ms: Ellesmere 1160.

Chapter III
"Ich am of Irlande." Ms: Rawlinson D.913, folio 1b.

"Tonight the snow is chilling" *(In-nocht is fúar in snechta).* Mss: RIA B iv 1; 23 K 44.

"Pangur Ban and I, each bent" *(Messe ocus Pangur bán).* Ms: From a ms in the Monastery of St. Paul in Carinthia.

"Bee flying fast, cup to cup" *(Daith bech buide a úaim i n-úaim).* Ms: TCD H.3.181 612a.

"Ah merle, merry you and well" *(Ach, a luin, is buide duit).* Ms: entered in the top margin of LB across p. 36.

"Wells of weeping, God me yield" *(A Dé, tuc dam topur ndér).* Ms: Franc ms A 9, p. 40.

"Wild wet waves are billowing" *(Tonna mora mórglana).* Pokorny, Reader, pp. 4-5.

"Dear each new thing, never dull" *(Gel cech núa – sásad nglé).* Ms: LL, folio 121a margin.

"Heart is he," *(Cride é).* Ms: BB.

"That fellow," *(Fil duine).* Mss: Rawl. B 502, folio 56r b 28, fac p. 99; LU, folio 7v (dip 512-517) ; TCD E.4.2, fol 26 a (Liber Hymnorum); YBL H 2.17, col 686.39 (fac, p. 75 a 40-42); Egerton 1782 (BM), folio 6v b 13; RIA C.3.2, folio 7r b 42.

Chapter IV
"Goats and farrows," Ms: Harl 5280, fol 42b. Translation by R.P.M. Lehmann. Included as stanzas 16-18 of "Guaire and Marban" in Lehmann's *Early Irish Verse* (p. 44).

"Merles make melody full well" *(Dom-farcai fidbaide fál).* Ms: St. Gall ms 904, lower margins.

"Starry King," *(A Rí rinn).* Mss: Br 5100-4; Franc ms A 9, p. 39.

"Be it sundown, be it dawn" *(In ba maiten, in ba fuin).* Mss: YBL, col 293-294 (across bottom margin); Laud 610, p. 411 a; and LB, p. 172.

"That fellow," see Chapter III.

Chapter V
"Mountain Snow." Previously unpublished translation by R.P.M. Lehmann.

"Summer's come, safe, sound" *(Táinic sam slán sóer).* Ms: Rawl. B 502, folio 59 b 2–60 a 1 (fac 106).

"Woman fair, to lands aglow" *(A bé find, in rega lim).* Mss: LU 131 b (dip 330.10814-10871); NLI 4.

"Arise, oh Ulster's fighter." From the "Sickbed of Cuchulainn." Ms: LU.

"See the warrior son of Lir" *(Fégaid mac láechraidi Lir).* Mss: LU 50 a 1 (dip 124.3959-4010); TCD H.4.22.

Chapter VI
"I have set my hert so hye." Ms: Bodl. Douce 381, f.20a

Chapter VII
"Here I am and fourthe I mouste." Ms: Bodl. Ashmole 1378, p. 60.

Chapter VIII
"Go to Rome" *(Techtdo Róim).* Ms: *Codex Boernerianus,* Munich.

Previously unpublished translation from the Welsh by R.P.M. Lehmann. Welsh text from *Canu Llywarch Hen*, "Prince-poet of the Cumbrian Britons."

Chapter IX
"Ware thee from the bere prey." Ms: Harley 7322.

Chapter X
"Swete Jesu, well may him be." Ms: Digby 86

Manuscript Abbreviations

BB:	*Book of Ballymote*
Franc:	Ms. formerly in the College of Irish Franciscans at Louvain, now at Killiney.
Harl:	Harleian ms, British Museum
Laud:	Laud ms, Bodleian Library, Oxford
LB:	*Leabar Breac*
LL:	*Book of Leinster*
LU:	*Lebar na hUidre (Book of the Dun Cow)*
Rawl:	Rawlinson ms, Bodleian Library, Oxford
RIA:	Royal Irish Academy
TCD:	Trinity College, Dublin
YBL:	Yellow Book of Lecan

Colophon

Five hundred copies of *Blessed Bastard*, by Ruth P. M. Lehmann, have been printed on 70 pound Nekoosa Linen natural paper, containing fifty percent recycled fiber, by Alpha & Omega Printing of Fort Worth, Texas. The cover was printed by Lopez Printing of San Antonio, Texas. The dust wrapper was printed on 80 pound Esse paper at San Antonio Press. Text was set in 11 point Bookman type, poems and titles in Meath.

Blessed Bastard was entirely designed and produced by Bryce Milligan, publisher, Wings Press.

The first fifty copies off the press were numbered, signed, and dated by the author.

Wings Press was founded in 1975 by J. Whitebird and Joseph F. Lomax as "an informal association of artists and cultural mythologists dedicated to the preservation of the literature of the nation of Texas." The current publisher/editor, Bryce Milligan, is honored to attempt to carry on that mission.